## MODERN CLASSICS
630

*Rumer Godden*

Rumer Godden (1907–98) was the acclaimed author of over sixty works of fiction and non-fiction for adults and children. Born in England, she and her siblings grew up in Narayanganj, India, and she later spent many years living in Calcutta and Kashmir. In 1949 she returned permanently to Britain, and spent the last twenty years of her life in Scotland. Several of her novels were made into films, including *Black Narcissus* in an Academy Award-winning adaptation by Powell and Pressburger, *The Greengage Summer*, *The Battle of the Villa Fiorita* and *The River*, which was filmed by Jean Renoir. She was appointed OBE in 1993.

# THE LADY AND THE UNICORN

## Rumer Godden

*Introduced by Anita Desai*

virago

VIRAGO

This paperback edition published in 2015 by Virago Press
First published in Great Britain in 1937 by Peter Davies

A CIP catalogue record for this book
is available from the British Library.

ISBN 978-1-84408-847-8

Typeset in Goudy by M Rules
Printed and bound in Great Britain by
Clays Ltd, St Ives plc

Papers used by Virago are from well-managed forests
and other responsible sources.

MIX
Paper from
responsible sources
FSC® C104740

Virago Press
An imprint of
Little, Brown Book Group
100 Victoria Embankment
London EC4Y 0DY

An Hachette UK Company
www.hachette.co.uk

www.virago.co.uk

# INTRODUCTION

An image that appears frequently in Rumer Godden's work, both fiction and autobiography – and the line between the two is a fine one – is that of a girl flying a paper kite, as she used to on the flat rooftop of her home in Bengal. In the memoir *Two Under the Indian Sun*, which she wrote with her sister Jon, she remembers:

> To hold a kite on the roller was to hold something alive ... something that kicked in your hand, that pulled up and sang as the string thrilled in the wind. The string went up and up until the kite seemed above the hawks circling in the sky; it linked us with another world, wider, far wider than ours.

The young heroine of *The River* declares, 'If it flies, I shall fly.' In both books the kite is used as a metaphor for childhood and the end of childhood. It might as well stand for her long and extraordinary life.

Rumer Godden was born in 1907 and died in 1998, so her life spanned almost the entire twentieth century. She lived through all its great upheavals – two world wars, the expansion of the British Empire, as well as its collapse – and through periods of personal joy and success, as well as struggle and betrayal. Throughout, she wrote with exemplary steadfastness. What gave a life, which had been volatile and dramatic, its core of stability, of serenity, even?

Two strands ran through it: one was her childhood in India at a time when the British ruled with a sense of security and the continuity of history; the other was her unwavering conviction of writing as her vocation. Towards the end, a third strand became apparent: a spiritual awareness that grew to a point where she felt able to commit to Catholicism. Throughout the twists and turns of a turbulent life, she retained the inner focus and belief of the child on the rooftop, holding the roller as her paper kite is lifted into the sky, allowing it the freedom of the winds, but maintaining her control.

Her father, Arthur Godden, in what Rumer Godden's biographer Anne Chisholm calls 'the high-Victorian heyday of the Empire', fought in the Boer War and then, bored at the prospect of settling down to life as a stockbroker in London, chose instead to work as an agent in one of the shipping companies based in Calcutta that ran steamers up and down the great rivers of the Gangetic delta. In *Two Under the Indian Sun* his life is described as one of adventure, excitement and a passionate attachment to the landscape of the riverine Bengal that Rumer was to inherit and cherish all her life. She described the childhood she and her three sisters shared at the house in Narayanganj, a small town beside a river, as 'halcyon', painting it in golden light, filling it with flowers and birds and imbuing it with all the comfort and security that could be provided by a large staff of servants – there were fifteen for a family of five. Education was certainly haphazard, provided by their maiden aunt Mary who lived with them, but Rumer grew up with a deep love of books and reading, which led quite naturally to an aptitude for writing. She first saw her writing in print at the age of twelve, in the Calcutta newspaper the *Statesman*, which confirmed her commitment to the writing life: always an imaginative child, she wrote under a pseudonym, assuming the role of a mother, and offered advice on how to keep children cool in the hot weather.

As the girls grew into adolescents, the Goddens decided to follow the British colonial tradition of taking their children back to England for a more conventional education. In 1920 the girls went with their mother to settle in Eastbourne where they learnt that the life of luxury and comfort they had taken for granted as members of the ruling class in India – the flag that was raised on their house at sunrise and lowered at sunset had them think of their home as Buckingham Palace – was over. Rumer found life in Eastbourne bleak and dreary, and suffered from the rigours of school life, going through as many as five in two years. It was in the last of them, Moira House, a progressive institution run by enlightened women, that the vice principal, Miss Swann, saw her literary talent and encouraged her writing. Swann was a writer herself and an exacting critic, but Rumer trusted her, and turned to her even as an adult for advice. One of the most beneficial exercises she gave Rumer was in précis: she had to reduce the leader of *The Times* to fourteen lines so that not a word was wasted. 'I owe her a tremendous debt,' said Rumer in later life.

No one in the family seems to have considered a university education as the next logical step. Instead, in 1925 their mother took them back to India with trunkfuls of new clothes to launch them in Calcutta society with its parties, dances, polo and riding. Rumer never felt comfortable in that social milieu and in 1927 she returned to London where, knowing she would have to support herself financially, she decided to train as a dancing teacher. She studied for two years and was offered a job on the staff, but instead went back to India to open her own dance school, first in Darjeeling and then in Calcutta. She rented premises in the best neighbourhood in the city and the school proved popular, particularly with the Eurasians of Calcutta. The British rather looked down on it for that very reason and there was gossip, hinting that Rumer must have Indian blood herself. She even received anonymous offensive letters and phone calls.

Of course, Rumer still belonged to the expatriate British society, and by this time she was married to Laurence Foster, a stockbroker, sportsman, and a popular figure in the exclusive Tollygunge Club circle. The couple honeymooned in Puri by the sea and nearly sixty years later she wrote a novel, *Coromandel Sea Change*, about an unhappy bride's realisation that she had made a mistake. It wasn't a marriage of minds or sensibilities, as was evident from her family's misgivings. In Calcutta she was expected to take part in Laurence's social life: 'for a while I tasted how beguiling it could be – as long as you stayed on the surface', but she remained critical of it: 'They were still in Britain, adapting their exile to as close a British pattern as they could, oblivious of everything Indian except for their servants.' *The Lady and the Unicorn* was born of this criticism of the common British disdain for Indians and Eurasians. She had already written a book called *Chinese Puzzle* about a Pekinese dog – she had a lifelong passion for the breed – which was published in 1935 when she was in England awaiting the birth of her daughter. It was not a commercial success but it gave her the opportunity to meet her publisher and agent in London. They had faith in her writing, which she took strength from when she returned to India.

Her third novel, *Black Narcissus*, published in 1939, was her first success – both commercial and critical. It was compared by Arthur Koestler to E. M. Forster's *A Passage to India* (which pleased Rumer, who said it was 'the book that changed my life') and turned into a movie. The film, which was enormously successful, disappointed Rumer but it did give her financial security and confidence.

Her marriage, on the other hand, went badly wrong. Her husband's career as a stockbroker failed and he joined the army, leaving Calcutta. Rumer, alone, took her two daughters to live in a small bungalow amidst the mountains and tea gardens of Darjeeling. This was a quiet, contemplative period of her life. She went for long walks and kept a diary that was later published as *Rungli-Rungliot* (subtitled 'Thus Far and No Further'). Next she went to live on a houseboat in Kashmir which was closer to where Laurence was posted, but his cantonment life and the company of soldiers' wives was no more attractive to her than expatriate society in Calcutta had been. Her marriage was effectively over. She moved to a small, basic cottage she called Dove House on a flowery hillside of streams and orchards.

Ultimately, this idyllic setting proved the scene of the most disturbing drama of her life: after the household fell ill and ground glass was found in the food, she became convinced they were being poisoned by the cook, Siddika. This could not be proved in court and he was acquitted but, ill and fearful, she left the place she had been happy and loved, and it would not be long before she would leave India for good. Many years later she wrote a fictionalised account in *Kingfishers Catch Fire*, which displayed her ability to write of the British in India with both intimate knowledge and a critical eye. The book was compared to Paul Scott's *The Jewel in the Crown* and, once again, to Forster's *Passage to India*. It was much less overtly political than either and its scope was narrower but it was an imaginative reconstruction of the colonial situation. As is evident from her novels, which often feature narrow-minded British characters, Rumer had ambiguous feelings about imperialism, but when Prime Minister Jawaharlal Nehru was quoted as saying 'My quarrel with the British is that they left a land of poverty-stricken wrecks,' she rose up in its defence and in 1944/45 she worked on a non-fiction book of the Women's Voluntary Service in Bengal, touring the various organisations it ran, and wrote with admiration of the good work it did.

One of these tours took her back to Narayanganj and, on seeing her old home, was moved to write a short autobiographical novel called *The River*. On reading it, the French director Jean Renoir immediately bought film rights, describing it as 'exactly the type of novel which would give me the best inspiration for my work ... an unexpressed, subtle, heartbreaking innocent love story involving a little girl.' They began a correspondence and Rumer helped him plan a trip with his wife to the site. On their return, he invited Rumer to Hollywood so they could work on the script together. 'Working with Jean was the best and richest year I've spent,' she later said. So different in character and background, the two became very close and held each other in high regard. Staying with the Renoirs, she met their friends the Chaplins, the Stravinskys, James Mason, Charles Laughton, Elizabeth Taylor and Greta Garbo, and hugely enjoyed the social life. When the script was ready to be filmed, she accompanied the crew to Bengal, sharing many decisions with the director. The film was shown at the Venice Film Festival in 1951 and won the International Critics' Prize, then opened in France and the USA to good reviews and is now regarded as a classic. Although the Indian press was rather critical of it, it had a premiere at the New Empire cinema in Calcutta that was attended by Prime Minister Nehru. Many of Godden's books were made into successful films in her lifetime, including Powell and Pressburger's famous adaptation of *Black Narcissus*; *Enchanted*, starring David Niven, which was based on *A Fugue in Time*; *The Battle of the Villa Fiorita*; *The Greengage Summer*; and *In this House of Brede*, but none of them brought her the satisfaction of *The River*.

Rumer divorced Laurence Foster, creating some turmoil for her daughters – which she later fictionalised in *The Battle of the Villa Fiorita* – and after filming *The River* she entered into a second, and very happy, marriage to James Haynes-Dixon, a civil servant who devoted himself to her and her career. Together they created a series of beautiful homes and gardens in London and in the countryside, including Lamb House in Rye, which was once the home of Henry James; her surroundings had always been very important to her.

In 1961 she made a new friend in Dame Felicitas Corrigan of Stanbrook Abbey in Worcestershire, and through her she established a link with the Benedictine order that led to her writing *In This House of Brede*, her longest, perhaps most complex novel, in which she strove to realistically depict convent life: many of the events were inspired by the nuns' own stories. In 1973 her husband died and a few years later she moved to a small house next to her daughter Jane's in Scotland, but she continued to write with her old regularity and determination. It was her habit to start a new book every New Year's

Eve and in her lifetime she completed an astonishing twenty-three novels, twenty-six books for children, fourteen books of non-fiction and seven collections and anthologies of poetry. In 1993 she was awarded the OBE.

This was not to be retirement for her. In 1994 the BBC planned a documentary on her life for the *Bookmark* programme and she was persuaded to travel with them to India for the last time for the making of the film. She returned to Bengal and even to Kashmir where she had sworn never to go again. It was an exhausting undertaking but at a farewell dinner she toasted the crew and told them that if she were a sensible old lady she would not have agreed to the journey and that she was glad she 'had never been sensible in her life'. She died four years later at the age of ninety and was buried next to her husband James in the old cemetery in Rye.

Rumer Godden knew both success and popularity in her life. Perhaps for that very reason she was troubled that she might be considered not a very serious but an entertaining, lightweight writer. She was also conscious of her own attractions to the whimsical and the precious, and the need to be on her guard and reserve that aspect for her many charming books for children. She never lost the child's fascination with the miniature but if there is any criticism that this prevented her from addressing the large events and political movements of her time, it does not hold; the miniature in her books contained, by reflection, the vastness of the world. This is surely the reason why her work has given so much pleasure to generations in many lands, and continues to do so.

Rumer Godden cannot be said to have been ignorant, or unmindful, of her society and its role in India. In no other

book is this made as clear as in *The Lady and the Unicorn*
which she wrote in the early, unhappy days of her first marriage. Running the dancing school in Calcutta had put her in
touch with Eurasians, and she wrote much of the book while
sitting on the verandah of the building, among the waiting
pupils, mothers and ayahs. This contact with the students,
their families and her staff taught her a great deal about the
unhappy situation of a community looked down upon both by
the English and by Indians as 'half-castes'. When the book
appeared, in 1937, the English thought she had been unfairly
critical of English society but others thought her depiction of
Eurasians was cruel. It was her publisher in England, Peter
Davies, who recognised its quality: he called it 'a little
masterpiece'.

In this book, Rumer Godden worked hard at looking at the
world she was living in, taking in both its romance and its
tawdriness. She did a great deal of research, exploring the
grand old mansions of East India Company days, many of
them crumbling and derelict; the Park Street cemetery where
many of the English of those times are buried in elaborate
graves and mausoleums; as well as the crowded, busy streets
behind New Market where the Eurasian community lived. In
describing a run-down, overcrowded house in that area, she
responded to its lingering romance – the fading frescoes on
the walls, the sun-dial covered in jasmine, the ghosts of a
weeping lady, a small dog and a horse carriage – but remained
alert to its disease-ridden drains, its rats and cockroaches, the
street outside with its chaotic traffic, its beggars and poverty.
Similarly, she saw the sadness in the hopeless aspirations of
girls like the Eurasian Lemarchant sisters, Belle and Rosa, but
also the reason why they were scoffed at by the English who

both courted them and despised them, like the young Englishman Stephen Bright, new to India and the Calcutta business world. He meets Rosa at what his colleagues call a 'B party':

'What's a B party?'
'A and B. B girls.'
'Oh, I see ... What happens?'
'Usual thing ... They behave very well and we behave very badly, and then they behave worse.'
'Oh!'

While the worldly-wise Belle understands the system and plays the game to her advantage, Rosa is hurt and can only reconcile herself to her family and circumstances when she sees Stephen's excitement on discovering that the sundial in her neglected, overgrown garden has the French inscription, *'Mon seul désir'*, which is linked to the *Dame à la Licorne* tapestries in the Musée de Cluny. This lends her a romantic appeal in his eyes, but he deplores that:

'You insist on being inferior Britons.'
'That isn't fair ... We are as much British subjects as you are.'
' ... It's all so false. You're no more like a British girl than that poinsettia is like a daisy. You talk of going home to England, when the only home you have is here in India. It's such a sham. Why can't you be content, more dignified?'

Finally the head of Stephen's firm informs him of the need to remember his place and keep them in theirs. Stephen is compelled to exclaim, 'God, what a muck heap this place is. Doesn't matter what you do if you're not serious, or what filth you commit to save your face.' 'Calcutta code,' his cousin William says pleasantly, 'You conform or go.' Everyone returns to the place where they belong; the code asserts itself. It is an unusual display of cynicism in Rumer Godden's work.

As in so much of her fiction, the seeds of this book lay in her childhood. Across the wall from the Godden house in Narayanganj there lived a Eurasian family, the Lafortes, whom they could watch from their rooftop. The Godden girls were fascinated by them but were not allowed to play with them for fear of being infected by their 'chi-chi' accents. The only time they could meet was at the annual Christmas party at the club she describes in *Two Under the Indian Sun*. It had taken all these years before she could write of that double sensation of fascination and fear.

*Anita Desai, 2014*

# I

Father Ghezzi had come to see father. Belle had done something that could not be told even to auntie; Blanche felt in every hair of her that it was something shocking.

The last time the priest came to see father was when Rosa had stolen the horse and cart out of the Christmas basket; there was always a basket in the church at Christmas to collect toys for the poor children. In those days the Lemarchants were so poor that really they should have had some of the toys, but that auntie would not allow. Belle and Rosa used to walk the streets at Christmas-time looking in the shop windows, yearning over their beauty, for they had no proper presents themselves until Rosa, tempted beyond endurance, took the horse and the cart.

She had been like that from a child, soft and easy to manage until her heart was set on something, and then implacable, almost ruthless, more like Belle than Rosa. She knew that it was wicked to steal, she felt it acutely, yet she had no compunction in stealing to get the horse and cart. When auntie said, 'You must tell Father Ghezzi you're sorry,' she had answered at once, 'If I tell him I'm sorry, will he let me keep the horse and cart?'

Auntie knew that it was sometimes like that with twins, that one should have slightly what the other showed strongly, just as one was always more vivid than the other, like a child and its reflection; not that Belle and Rosa were children any more or at all alike, but Rosa always seemed a shadow by her sister, and that, auntie thought, was why Father Ghezzi and the nuns at school scarcely seemed to notice her.

The Lemarchant children had known the priest all their lives. He had baptized them, and Belle had always been his favourite. All they saw of Belle at school was her down-dropped lids with their honey-coloured lashes, her pretty hands and her neat red head. They had given her a medal for goodness. That made even Rosa smile; for good conduct, yes, but for goodness, no.

Her own family were sure that Belle was not good, and yet at home she gave hardly any trouble; it was just that she was quite implacable, quite determined and almost fearless. Auntie never forbade her to do anything, for she knew it was useless, Belle did exactly as she chose. When she was crossed she was more than unkind, she was shocking, and none of them were really good enough for Belle.

Among the friendly litter of slippers and brushes and powder and pins and old bottles in the bedroom, Belle kept her things separate; no one was allowed to use her nail polish or the face-creams and powder she bought with her prize-money, no one was allowed to borrow the sets of underclothes she had made herself from soft voile. She kept the handkerchiefs she picked up at school and unpicked the name-tapes, and would not let auntie cut up even her old knickers for her little sister Blanche.

Her friend at school was Miriam Rambert of the bold eyes. They went into corners and whispered and refused to tell Rosa what they said. Father Ghezzi, who confessed the girls, tried to separate them. 'He is afraid of your bad influence,' said Belle, and laughed.

'My bad influence!' cried Miriam, and for once she was indignant.

Belle could charm even auntie, who knew the worst of her; however angry she was, Belle made her laugh when she mimicked Father Ghezzi or Mother Celia with her bunion, or the pin-man asking for his money or Mrs Barton putting on airs; but when it came to her taking the Blessed Virgin in the tableaux, auntie was shocked.

'No! No! that cannot be,' she said, and put on her hat to go and see Father Ghezzi.

'Couldn't it be Rosa?' she asked timidly. Little Rosa with her still face might very well have taken the Blessed Virgin in auntie's eyes, but Father Ghezzi thought her uninteresting and began to talk of Belle's fine character.

'But Rosa has a lovely nature,' pleaded auntie.

'Rosa tells lies,' said the Father severely. It was so. Rosa could never be quite truthful, she had always to distort, to embroider, to exaggerate, and if she were frightened, she lied.

Auntie did not think that telling lies was a bad fault, anyhow not so uncomfortable as taking the only bath-towel or interrupting when people were saying their prayers.

'Apart from that she has a lovely nature,' she said again.

'Then you need not be jealous for her, Mrs Kempf. Remember that it is after careful thought that we have chosen Belle. You should be proud for her to appear as the Holy Virgin.'

'You should hear her speak of the Holy Virgin when she is out of temper,' thought Auntie, and sighed and came home.

Now Father Ghezzi had come to them and, as he waited in

the sitting-room while Boy helped father to put on his tie and coat, and auntie changed her slippers for shoes behind the partition, he seemed very uneasy and sad.

He had an umbrella of holland lined with green against the heat; it looked womanish and strange with the cassock and square-toed boots; he had not gone into white although the heat was intense, and his clothes were dusty and stained. The light from the veranda fell on his face, thinly drawn and sensitive; his beard gave him a gallant Spanish look, though Belle said it made him look like a goat.

Mr Lemarchant came in, himself a little uneasy, as he always was with the priest; he waited, but Father Ghezzi seemed unable to say a word, he remained sorrowful and perplexed, as if he were pleading to be understood without having to put it into words.

Father fidgeted and said: 'You will let Anna order you some tea? You will take tea with us, eh?'

As if he had not heard, the priest burst out: 'I don't know which it is that is worse to have in this country, Mr Lemarchant, boys or girls, sons or daughters. With the sons it is one thing; they cannot get work, the Indians squeeze them out from beneath, the English from above, so—' He brought his clenched hands together as if he were crushing a poor little man to death. 'They cannot get work; before they begin they are failures. And with the girls it is another thing, they are too successful. Yes. There is always success for these girls, so smart, so nimble, so empty-headed. They take even the jobs the boys might have; they go into offices, shops, and what happens? They get money, they get ideas, they are taken up by men – men in Calcutta society, faugh! – and then when they are in trouble they are flung back on their people; on those boys whose place they have taken, boys for whom they have now no use and who could not marry them if they had.'

'Yes, yes,' said father, 'but I don't understand, what has this to do with me?'

'It has everything to do with you,' said Father Ghezzi, in his careful and measured English. 'Of all the pupils, Mr Lemarchant, Belle was the one I was most certain of. I said she had a fine character, but I was deceived. I was blind, Mr Lemarchant, she is a bad girl. We have talked together, the Mother Superior and I, you can imagine how grieved we are to do this, but we have spoken to Belle and she has not listened to us; I have come to tell you, Mr Lemarchant, that we think it is better that she should leave school now, and not wait for the holidays.'

'But the holidays are only two months away. Think of the shame of it, Father.'

'We have to think of the other pupils, Mr Lemarchant.'

'But what has she done? You haven't told me what she has done.'

Father Ghezzi hesitated. 'It is difficult to put into words, but it has become quite impossible for us to keep her.'

'But what has she done? What has she said?'

There was a pause. 'She has actually done nothing,' said the priest slowly. 'She has, actually, said nothing. She has behaved exactly as she has always behaved, but with a difference! It is her attitude, an attitude of mockery, if I have to say it, of diabolical mockery. A terrible change has come over her. She was so quiet, so modest, and now she seems to taunt us.

'Yesterday, in church, during the Sacrament, Mr Lemarchant' (each word was a groan) 'I had put the wafer on her tongue and she attracted my attention. At that moment, Mr Lemarchant, you cannot believe it, but it is true, and she looked—'

How could he describe that look? He had not ceased to see it since that moment.

The deep severe trance, the reverent ecstasy, a young girl might feel them both; he had seen them blush, quiver, pale and faint: he had known them grow self-conscious, have silly talk among themselves, be conscious of the priest as a man, and that had been shocking enough, but there was a worse taunt in Belle's look, and even now he shrank from it. She had looked at him, he could hardly say it even to himself, not as if she desired him but he her; and she had calculated it, she had chosen that moment, the highest – he could not go on. It was blasphemy, and he said it aloud.

'It was blasphemy!' He tried to speak quietly. 'It was blasphemy, Mr Lemarchant.'

'Certainly it was,' said father, who had no idea what had happened. 'I am very annoyed that one of my children has committed blasphemy and I shall punish her. I promise you.'

'It is a matter of more than that. You understand that she must leave the school, and we think her sister Rosa should leave with her, Mr Lemarchant, for they are so much together. They must be watched. You must explain to Mrs Kempf. Belle must be sent to see me, she must make a regular confession. It is a question of her soul.'

'Yes, yes,' protested father. 'I shall see to it, certainly I shall see to it.'

The priest seemed to grow old as he sat in his chair, and his eyes as they looked at father were tired. For fifty-one years he had been dealing with these people, these facile Anglo-Indians, and he was tired and sad. It was like digging in sand, you could not get to the bottom of their contradictions, their cross-purposes. It was their blood, the contempt of one part for another; the contempt of the Britisher for the native he rules, a contempt that runs like cold pure metal through the easy

tissues of the native indolence and shiftlessness, pleasant dis-
honesty and inconsequence; and the resentment of the Indian
under that domination, his fight for freedom that is alien to his
element of content, of settlement and culture if he could but
find peace.

Peace. There could be no peace for these people who must
always be against the winning side, no matter which side wins,
carrying in themselves their certainty of defeat. For them a place
would always have to be made, they could call no place their
own; and while he fumed over their behaviour, he marvelled at
their courage.

Mr Lemarchant shifted uneasily in his chair, Father Ghezzi
stirred himself, sat up and said, 'You must send her to see me.
You must watch her, I solemnly warn you . . . '

After he had gone, Belle came out of the bedroom, where she
had listened to every word, while auntie whispered to herself
that when children were no longer children they became
exceedingly tiresome. Belle was eating nuts which she cracked
between her teeth.

'Why were you hiding?' stormed father. 'Did you hear what he
said?'

'I did,' said Belle.

'Why did you do it, what he said you did?'

'Because it amused me, I think,' said Belle, considering. 'It
was something I've wanted to do for a very long time.'

'Now you will have to leave school, you and Rosa as well.
Think of the disgrace. What do you say to that?'

'I say it's a good thing,' said Belle. 'I've done with school. I made
them want to keep me there and now I've made them want to
send me away. Isn't it funny, father,' she added dreamily, 'that I can
make those old wise good people do exactly what I want?'

Auntie, who was listening behind the partition, shook her head and crossed herself.

Father was angry with Belle, and if he had looked out of the window he would have been angrier still, for he would have seen Rosa with Robert deSouza in the garden, under the palms that rustled like paper in the wind.

Rosa was twenty minutes younger than her twin sister Belle, and since she was fourteen she had been in love with Robert. She had to love someone, and Robert was more beautiful even than his beautiful brothers and sisters, olive-skinned, with hair dark and plumy and eyes like blue diamonds. She had not said anything about it until one evening after school when she had nothing to do but wander in the garden; Robert had begun to walk there too, lingering after dark, and they talked in a polite manner, which was odd considering that they lived in the same house and had known each other for most of their lives; and Robert suddenly confessed he was in love.

'In love?' said Rosa, and her anxiety seemed to tear the words from her. 'Oh! Robert, who with?'

'With you,' said Robert simply, and the stars swung out of their places and back again, leaving Rosa dizzy and breathless.

They had wanted to take Robert for a priest at his Jesuit school, his look of beauty and obedience had marked him out; the priest said he had a vocation, but he had refused.

'How else do you think you'll live?' asked Mr deSouza, his father. 'What else can you do? There is nothing in India for boys like you and I cannot send you to Europe. All of you,' he cried, turning to his swarm of sons and daughters, 'all of you had better be priests and nuns.'

'Robert won't be a priest, because he wants to marry Rosa Lemarchant,' said Eileen spitefully.

'Now you hear me, Bob,' roared Mr deSouza. 'There will be nothing of that. You'll marry no one unless I tell you. The Lemarchants are not a nice family at all, they cannot even pay their rent, so that I am always out of pocket; and not only must I keep you when money is scarce, but keep your wife as well.'

'Poor father,' said little Bruce, 'perhaps one day you'll have some money.'

'What do you mean, poor father,' said Mr deSouza indignantly. 'I have plenty of money.'

Robert thought night and day of how he could marry Rosa.

At seventeen she was in full flower, the moon-flowers of the east that bud for a night; her skin was as pale as their petals, her eyes dark shadowed. She was small, almost flimsy, very proud of her tiny hips, and pitied Belle for her larger measurements. Belle was not jerry-built like her sisters, she had curves, swelling into her waist and firm pointed breasts; the others might have had pith in their bones instead of blood, but her skin was the rich cream that sometimes goes with red hair. She had her hair from father, like flame silk, the colour of sacred marigolds. Rosa's hung to her shoulders, and she wore it in a plait over her head as Blanche wore her celluloid bandeau.

'I wish mine was a plait, then I could hardly lose it,' sighed Blanche, for at school and with auntie it was always, 'Blanche Lemarchant, you untidy child, where *is* your bandeau?'

Blanche was the family shame, for she was dark. Suddenly, after Belle and Rosa, had come this other baby like a little crow after twin doves. Auntie said she was like their mother, and they hated to think of their mother who was dead and had been dark like Blanche. Belle could not bear her, and even Rosa was ashamed to be her sister.

They must have had hill-blood, for Blanche had the high

cheek-bones and eyes of a little Chinese from the outer Mongolian-Thibetan fringes of her ancestry, and she had their merriment and simplicity in pleasure until she was teased or upset.

None of them ever mentioned their mother, yet she had given to all her children a courage that father did not possess and that she must have needed in her life with him. With her skin she had given the most of her courage to Blanche, who would face even father if she were angry.

'God help you with that awful temper,' auntie would say.

But to balance her courage she had nerves, worse than Rosa; often after a fight with father she had to go into the bathroom and vomit down the pan.

Father had been so very handsome, auntie told them, but now the top button of his trousers could not do up, the back of his neck was fat, and among his curly hair was a bald patch.

'But you must remember,' said auntie, 'that we owe everything to your father. Poor father, he has worked so hard.'

Blanche simply did not believe it; she had known father for nine years and never yet seen him do any work.

He bought old refrigerators and sewing machines and bicycles that no one could use and took them to pieces all over the sitting-room, to put them together again with new parts he had invented, and usually no one could use them still. Presently Boy would put them out in the godown and father would say that he had been cheated, and he was buying something else that would sell for three hundred rupees and pay off everything he owed.

The godown could have been let as a garage, but he was too lazy to clear it out. He smoothed his hair and said, 'No, no. I do not care to earn money that way.'

There were so many ways that father did not care to earn

money that the girls had to be taken at school for charity and the rent was always owing to Mr deSouza, who always wanted to be paid on the regular day.

Boy was the only person who could deal with father; when he was drunk and went to sleep with his head on the table, Boy pulled him off his chair into the bedroom and threw him down on the bed and took off his shoes and trousers; he was the only person who dared to touch his machines or get money from him for the housekeeping.

Boy did not know how old he was, but he had only a few sparse hairs left in his beard, his hands shook so that he dropped plates and dishes continually, and he had a cataract in one eye. He was a Mussulman, and every evening he would put down the work he was doing and take his mat into the garden and say his prayers. Although he was rough to father when he was drunk, Boy treated him with the same honour that auntie did, an honour that was blind and unreasoning and persistent; no matter how badly he behaved they treated him as the honourable head of the house, and auntie complained that the children did not respect him as they ought.

The more auntie worked the fatter she grew and the more her feet and ankles swelled. 'Work your fingers to the bone,' it said, but auntie's had gone the other way; now they were so fat that they had quite lost their shape, the nails were ground down and she could hardly see her wedding ring, though it was a wide one, all she had left to show that she was Mrs Kempf and that there had once been an Adolf Kempf who had loved her and married her when she was not as old as Belle and Rosa were now.

'I was sixteen,' said auntie, 'and he left me before I was twenty, and now I am fifty-eight! I don't think,' she added, 'that he'll come back.'

Meanwhile she went on keeping the house and looking after the children, and going to the market and cutting down clothes and worrying over money and Blanche's stomach and putting up with father, not knowing if she were happy or not, because the days were all the same and she had little time in them to think. Only when she saw something that reminded her, a white ribbon flying in the wind like a wedding streamer, or the shade of cerise that had been the colour of her parasol, or heard a sentimental tune, would she have a stab of memory and, if it was very late or she was tired, she might weep, but not for long. She was so accustomed now to being auntie that nothing else was real, and she would talk about Mrs Kempf as if she were a rich relation, someone she had been proud to know, and not herself. She told Blanche stories of her.

'Mrs Kempf had a white feather boa and then Mr Kempf came one day with a roll of silk from England, and it was watered.'

'You mean it was wet?' said Blanche.

'It was not wet,' said auntie, 'in the silk was a pattern of water and it was mauve. The tailor was to make a costume, and on the edges were three rows of braid, and what do you think? There was not enough braid, and the owl of a tailor, he cut the edges and tightened the sleeves so that the braid would go round, and when he brought it, Mrs Kempf could not put it on at all. There was Mr Kempf waiting to go out and Mrs Kempf in her hat and no dress and the boa . . .'

Since she had gone to school Blanche did not want to listen to auntie any more; all the time she was after the deSouzas and auntie was left alone. She had no one to talk to, and soon she began to talk to herself.

In the evenings, when she sat in her rocker on the veranda,

she was so tired that her body felt like a bag that had been thrown about all day, and her feet burned even in her Chinese slippers, but still she had to talk; and, because she knew that none of the others would listen, that their thoughts and the things they wanted to say were so much more important than her own, she talked under her breath, only moving her lips as she sat, and it was too dark for them even to see that. She suffered terribly from her feet. One of the sisters had said, 'Really, Mrs Kempf, on these stone floors one's feet are like boils at the end of the day. Regular boils!' That was how auntie always thought of them now, as boils inside her shoes. 'Regular boils,' she said, and somehow that comforted her. Every now and then a crash came from the pantry. She screamed, 'Boy! Boy! What are you doing? What have you broken? I'll cut your pay, Boy.' Boy answered, 'Issoup plate, memsahib,' or 'Pudding bowl, memsahib.' He broke so much crockery that if auntie had remembered the cuts she gave him he would never have had any wages at all.

They sat out on the veranda on those Calcutta evenings and watched the afternoon light grow rich and deep in the garden, where the grass turned to emerald and the trees seemed to dip down and draw their colour from the grass. The canna lilies shone pink and scarlet in parrot colours, and close, in pots by the steps, were picotees, the white with crimson edges that smell the sweetest of all.

It was March, and even that garden that was not kept at all had its lilies and its colours; the flowers from the bauhinia tree had fallen romantically on the grass and the jasmine over the old broken stones was in bud. Presently the night would come, when the garden sank away and the palm trees like ships sailed against the sky, when the colours were lost and only the scents were left, stronger and sharper because it was night.

If there was a moon, Rosa loved to watch the coming of the moonlight into the quiet garden that was turned away from the house of noise and laughter. In the moonlight the garden opened like a flower, disclosing its petals of light one by one, until it had opened quite and shown its dark heart to the moon and the moon had turned it pale. Rosa met Robert secretly in the garden, and with each other they were quiet and a little mysterious, and she filled him with a lighted happiness, as if he were the garden and she were the moon.

## 2

From the old burying grounds, Park Street turns down to the maidan that is spread between Chowringhee and the river; in flat spaces of green it runs between borders of flowering trees, from the Memorial with its domes and flying Victory rising into the air, to the grassed hummocks of the Fort and the gates of Government House.

Park Street is the border line. To the south the streets draw away, wide and shaded between garden houses, to Ballygunge and Alipore, before they congest again to the Indian quarter, but to the north they are an intricate web, threads of lanes and alleys between the roaring central streets where the traffic runs far into the night.

In those backstreets are hives of houses, lost and forgotten from old Calcutta, and there, among derelict rooms and gardens built over with shops and garages and shoddy blocks of flats, live the poor Anglo-Indian community. There are a few houses, closed in their garden walls, clean and cherished, where the family have lived for decades, Armenians, Jews, or domiciled Anglo-Indians, wealthy and proud; but for the most part the houses that still stand intact on their ground have fallen from their station and are let in flats and suites, housing a dozen families where once they had housed one.

The house where the Lemarchants lived, at the corner of the lane beyond the market, was one of these, a house that rose up high and narrow in its garden. It was not like the houses of John Company days, thick-walled, with pillared verandas and high chunam-washed walls; it might rather have come from a Provençal town, yellow-plastered with blue painted shutters and scrolled iron balconies. It had no verandas, and on every floor was a vast echoing vestibule; from each the far ceiling could be seen, topping the second flight, a ceiling painted with a hunting scene.

The colours had faded and the rain soaked in, but still the horses cantered down the dim spaces, by woods and hillocks of sage-green grass, ridden by gentlemen and simpering ladies whose habits flowed like waterfalls to the ground. The stag was in the corner over the well of the stairs, springing to the rocks, his antlers lowered in challenge to the hounds, a dun-coloured pack half blotted out; the greens and the creams and the browns had mingled with the damp, mottled and patched with mildew, so that it was hard to tell the painted scene from the shapes that had come there with the years. Blanche declared that the figures moved, that in season the trees turned brown and green or bare, and she loved to lie in bed at night and think of them; the company and the huntsmen, the hounds and horses and the stag, who need not fear for he never could be caught, chasing through those glades and across the feathered grass, and if she strained to hear she thought that once or twice she caught the faint note or a horn.

There was not a corner of the house that Blanche did not

know and cherish, all of them loved it as if it were their own; that was peculiar to the Lemarchants, for the house did not like its tenants, it seemed to have some strange resentment, especially against the deSouzas. Even Mr deSouza, who would say 'Tcha! Don't talk to me of such nonsense' over any such idea, had an uneasy feeling that the house did not like him and had not liked his father or his grandfather; it had brought them bad luck, their fortune was certainly gone and now a kind of feud had sprung up between them. If Mr deSouza could spoil and degrade the house, he did, and it had a way of retaliating; it thwarted him, he hated it and wanted to be rid of it.

He remembered the wall-paper in the bedroom; some of the rooms were papered, and in those upstairs a few of the papers had survived. They were valuable and he had sold one, a Chinese pattern in blue and white; but when they came to take it off the wall it clung and would not come away, and when at last they stripped it off, it fell into powder and he had to give the money back.

His tenants were endlessly asking for repairs, only the Lemarchants were content; from the first day that he had persuaded them to crowd into the annex they had been happy. To tell the truth it was not in a fit state to let to anyone. He had taken out the panelling and sold it, there was nothing but a native earth oven in the pantry and the ceiling cloth was nearly rotten, yet they never had any complaints. He despised them a little for that, but he had a curious feeling about them, as if he should have offered them a first floor suite, as if he would have been wise if he had invited them to live in it, as if it would have placated the house in some way to have the Lemarchants living in its best rooms, which was absurd, for they could hardly pay the rental of the annex.

Auntie's were the only flowers that grew in the garden, since she had come it had taken on a miraculous life, even the old dried bushes had flowered again under her care.

Now the house seemed to be giving way; defeated by its own decay, it was dying. The years of robbery and neglect and squeezing had choked its life away; now it seemed that it could not help troubling the Lemarchants, dropping flakes of plaster from the ceiling on their furniture, blocking their drains, letting the damp creep along their walls, and all the while it was mutely apologetic, pleading forgiveness for its bad manners as some old ill gentleman distresses himself when he cannot behave as he would in public.

It was very old. Once coaches had driven through the gate, and carriages swaying on their springs so that the footmen swayed too, under the umbrella they held over the bell-shaped muslins below; the umbrella dipped and swayed between the flower beds and the strange foreign creepers and Indian sky, it had a golden fringe and the horses wore fly-nets of silver. The gold and silver had tarnished long ago, the gates were shut, the bolts stuck with dirt and rust, but there was a story in the bazaar that a carriage still went out, driving through the double doors as if they were mist, and the sound of horses' hooves went galloping away down the street.

'Is the house haunted then?' the tenants asked Mr deSouza when they came to view a suite that had fallen empty. They were always falling empty and the people complaining that the whole house was rotten; there were white ants in the woodwork, damp in the walls and the drains were blocked up and smelt.

Mr deSouza was not disconcerted. He still pointed his toes in his elegant boots, his suits were still of tussore silk and the rims of his pince-nez of gold, and he had the same curious scent which came from the caraway seeds he ate and the attar of roses he used. The only beautiful thing about Mr deSouza was the zircon he wore in his little finger-ring, it was a clear blue and as brilliant as a diamond; he himself was very ugly, yet he had eleven children each more lovely than the last. They had a peculiar ripeness, a bloom on their skins like fruit; their hair and their lashes were luscious and curly, their eyes softly black or as blue and brilliant as the zircon, and they had Irish or Scottish names – Robert, Colleen, Eileen, Pat and Bruce – that did not match with deSouza at all. Their father's name was Casimiro Alarico, and he smacked their heads when he was angry, even Robert who was twenty-one, and none of them ever answered back. Mrs deSouza had given up long ago; the children were not looked after at all and had every kind of bad habit.

In the days of their grandfather, another Alarico deSouza, the house had not been cut up into flats, but they now lived on the top floor and let the others out in suites; as many people as possible were crowded into each floor, even the annex that was one long room had been partitioned into three and held the whole Lemarchant family. They all went in and out by a door cut into the great gates which had not been used for years.

When the Lemarchants first came to the house Mr deSouza had been very polite. He put up another partition to cut a cubicle off the bedroom for father to sleep in, and built on the veranda, making one of the windows into a door.

The annex was at the eastern side of the house with the garden on the same side; it had an entrance from the vestibule through a low passage and a pointed door, but chiefly they used the veranda door where auntie kept her pots of flowers. The one long room was partitioned into a sitting-room and bedroom and father's cubicle; the roof was arched, Mr deSouza had put in the ceiling of cloth with a wash of plaster that crumbled off now in a fine dust so that it was difficult to keep the rooms clean. There were arches over the windows too, and at each apex a carving of a shield and a four-legged beast that might have been a leopard with a spear plunged in its head.

'What is it?' they asked.

'Some decoration. I don't know,' said Mr deSouza.

Blanche was passionately interested in animals; she wondered often what the carving could be. 'It isn't a dog, is it, Rosa? And why has it a spear in its head? I think it's a tiger that has just been killed.'

'It has no stripes,' said Rosa, 'so it must be a leopard.'

'It has no spots,' countered Blanche, 'so it might be a tiger, and it might be a rhinoceros with a horn on its forehead, but it isn't that kind of a shape. It isn't any kind of shape really, so perhaps it could be a dog.'

More than anything in the world she wanted a dog of her own, a dog or any kind of an animal.

'Father, can I have a dog?' But she could never have anything from father.

'A canary, then?'

'Where will you get the money for a canary?'

'Well, can I have a guinea pig? They're only fourteen annas.'

'You can't have a guinea pig,' roared father. 'You've nowhere to keep it.'

'Well, I *shall* have a goldfish,' said Blanche rebelliously. 'I have that much money, and I shall keep it in a soup-plate.'

There were no carvings over the windows of the main house, nor were they arched; they were the oblong windows of most Indian houses, with slatted wooden shutters. The house was too high for the garden and the porch too large for the house, an immense porch with fluted columns and a sweep of marble steps. From the vestibule the staircase rose in a spiral, the stairs seen from beneath were like the sticks of a fan, spreading up one above the other to the second floor, and in the centre of the ground-floor vestibule was a shallow basin, carved with spirals and flowers of white marble that had once been a fountain. Mr deSouza had sold the central figure, but the basin was fixed to the floor, and it was so wide that it could hardly have been taken out through the doors; it was used for rubbish and litter, the servants spat in it and the washermen rested their bundles on it before they climbed the stairs.

All up the stairs were niches, and on the landings the doors were high and of fine-grained wood, but the tenants had painted them in various colours and fastened their name plates into the wood; the names changed so often that the doors were riddled with screw holes. On every landing the servants congregated, squatting and talking or playing cards.

The rooms were built in suites, large and small rooms leading from one another; they were high and spaced, some with floors of fitted wood, some chequered in marble, their ceilings were moulded with grapes and scrolls and wreaths on ribbons. The walls were papered, except where the tenants had asked for them to be colourwashed over; the papers were fitted to the walls with decorations of gilt, the white ants had eaten them nearly away and cockroaches fed on the paper. There were still the marks of candle sconces along the walls, and on the pillars in the porch were sockets of iron for torches.

The drive, that ran only a few yards from the gate to the porch, was nearly as wide as it was long, more like a court than a driveway; down one side Mr deSouza had built a row of corrugated-iron garages and sheds, opening on to the road, and facing the porch was a dirty back-yard where the car-cleaners threw the water and the children liked to play better than in the garden. Cassia trees grew along the drive, hiding the tin roofs when they were in leaf, and dropping their petals among the refuse on the ground, and the petals were of so vivid a colour that the children used to gather them to play at cooking fires.

There was a lawn in the garden, and thickets of poinsettias, oleanders, and dusty hibiscus, a bauhinia, and a frangipani tree. The flower-beds were grassed over except for the bed of canna lilies and the flowers that bloomed from auntie's packets; but there were still the palms planted in two lines to make an avenue leading to an old stump of masonry that the jasmine had overgrown.

'What is that?' people asked.

'Some rubbish. I don't know,' said Mr deSouza.

He meant one day to remove it and make a tennis court to send up the rent of his flats, but after all these years there was still no tennis court. Auntie had hoped that the jasmine would be taken away; it brought sorrow, she said, and would not have it in the house.

The noises of the backstreet came over the wall; motor-horns and wheels and horses' hooves, the bicycle bells on the rickshaws and the bicycle bells on the bicycles and the endless hum and chatter of people's voices; people spitting and hawking, and blowing their noses with their fingers, laughing, crying or splashing water from the street tap, or working Singers in the tailors' shops.

There was a nest of carpenters' shops where they made useless little chairs and tables for children and native string beds, and the De Luxe Edition, which was a restaurant for soldiers from the Fort, a place that auntie would not allow the girls into, and there were tailors' shops like boxes in a row, opening on the street with the tailors sitting on the floor around a dummy, holding their seams with their big toes. Over the tailors lived Mrs Anthony, the Madrassi ayah, who went to help poor women with their births; when the girls met Mrs Anthony in the street, as she salaamed them, she would look at their hips as if she were measuring them, and thinking that Belle might do, but Rosa was too narrow to be good for anything.

The pin-man who washed and cleaned dresses next door to the Model Girls' Academy had been owed his money since Christmas; now he would not take away pinwashing unless the money was paid in advance, and would call out to auntie and Rosa as they passed or stop Blanche as she went to school.

'To-morrow, to-morrow. Come to-morrow and you will be paid,' Blanche muttered with burning cheeks, but she knew and they knew that to-morrow would be a long time coming.

Beyond the Academy was the Ruby Hardware Store with a sign hanging out above that said 'Mad Cure, Madnesses, Fits and Excitements cured here, also Measles and Pox and Impotence. Come and try. Female diseases guaranteed.'

Through the door in the front gate the people could be seen passing by on the pavement; a man carrying bassinets on a pole, and two Sikh women who held their veils across their noses, and one of them had a birdcage with a cover of magenta gauze with tassels; a Chinaman in grey cotton selling embroidered linen, a widow in dirty white on her way to the street tap, and three coolies carrying baskets of marigold garlands on their heads.

In the first hours of the morning the carts came creaking past on their way to market, and all the rest of the day odds and ends of vegetables lay in the road, cabbage stalks and potatoes and lady's fingers, and some were thrown into the garden so that the most surprising vegetables were found on the lawn. Belle wrinkled up her nose when she found them, and lifted them up with a stick and threw them back over the wall. Blanche gathered them up and took them to auntie, who put them in the soup, for how else could she give them vegetables with the prices so high in the market? She told Blanche all the same that her ways were low.

Blanche knew every shop and most people in the street, and about everyone in the house, even the Bengali family on the first floor who were friends with no one else, even the ever-changing tenants of the flats next door to them; they had not been taken a week before Blanche could tell you the history of every person in them.

Mr Kawashima, the Japanese gentleman who taught jiu-jitsu, had no children and no wife, only strange Japanese ladies in short European dresses who visited him at night after his pupils had gone. There were always thuds and noises coming from his suite, and Belle said he must make love as violently as he taught jiu-jitsu. Auntie said he was not respectable, but he had a happy lemon-coloured face, and on his birthday he had a cake made of strings of sugar knotted and bundled like straws, stuck with paper figures of ladies with flowers in their hair and nothing else on at all.

The Mascarenes in suite number two were worse off than the Lemarchants; in their partitioned room they had the baby *and* the band. Between the band practising and the baby crying and Mrs Mascarenes scolding, the other tenants were always complaining to Mr deSouza, who came down and complained to Mr Mascarenes.

Mr Mascarenes was small and pleading, with a wax-white face and little hands; he could not get engagements for his band, he was always a minute too late for the chance of a long engagement, or just missing by a hair a wonderful offer, and then he had to come back and break it to his band, which had practised so diligently while he was away. People complained of the noise, Mrs Mascarenes scolded, and the baby, who was eighteen months and could not yet stand, lay in his tan-sad with his eyes shut, his hair in a fringe like Mr Kawashima's, his little wax fingers curled in his shawl, and cried and cried and cried.

'He needs cod liver oil for his legs and can't have it, poor thing,' said Blanche. 'I think he will die.'

The most important family were the Bartons. They had the whole west side of the ground floor to themselves, and only stayed there because Mr Barton had built an aviary and was obstinate and would not leave it.

When you went near Mr Barton you became at once quiet and refined, for he treated you like a grown-up lady, or if you were grown up already, like a queen. Every time you went there he showed you his birds, and even if you were not interested, you felt honoured; even Belle did not laugh at him, though he wore funny clothes, carpet slippers and a shawl in the cold weather. But she called Mrs Barton a silly peacock.

For years and years Mrs Barton had prayed and prayed, and at last God had sent her a little baby called Désirée.

'How did you know she was called Désirée?'

'She was named when she came.'

'But how did you *know*? Was she labelled?'

If Mrs Barton was like a peacock, Désirée was like a little starved donkey with big ears and wavering legs, which was strange, because the Bartons had a great deal of money for cod liver oil; Désirée's hats were bought at Wall and Robinson's, her combinations were Chilprufe, and she was going to school in England.

She showed Blanche a picture that looked rather like the Sibpore Engineering College stuck on a gaunt hill.

'The girls all wear blue stockings,' she told Blanche.

'Blue *stockings*!' cried Blanche. She was far more amazed at their wearing stockings at all than at the stockings being blue.

Auntie was impressed, and wanted Blanche to play with Désirée. 'It was Jean deSouza who taught you to pick your nose, Blanche. Why can't you play with a nice child like Désirée?'

If she could not play with the deSouzas, Blanche sat with Boy in the pantry. They made charms. If you dropped melted tea-lead into cold water it told what your husband might be; a sword for a soldier, a fish for a fisherman, money for a merchant. Blanche always had some curious objects that might have been anything at all. Boy could open soda water bottles with his thumb and told stories about ghosts.

'This house is haunted!' she shrilled. 'Do you really say that, Boy?'

'It is haunted,' said Boy in a sepulchral voice, removing a piece of their chutney from his beard. 'There is a carriage that drives away from this house and through the gates as if they were not there, and you can hear horses galloping down the road, and there is lightning under their feet that will strike a man dead, and none of the horses have any heads ... '

'I *don't* believe it,' said Blanche, her eyes like saucers. 'I think if you met them you would just think they were ordinary horses, Boy.'

'Well, you tell it yourself then,' said Boy angrily, spitting on the Blanco to clean father's shoes.

# 3

Father had hired the typewriter. It stood menacingly on the sideboard, and Belle and Rosa were to take turns at it.

'But how can they do it without instruction?' asked auntie.

'They must sit at it until they can,' said father. 'What laziness! Did anyone teach me engineering, I ask you? How did I learn to repair my machines?'

Auntie was silent, for not even she could say that father repaired his machines.

Belle liked the idea of typing, she had picked out a letter already, but to Rosa it was tragic.

'You have to know shorthand and speed and all sorts before you can go in an office,' she cried. 'I'm not going to be made a fool.'

'Oh, I shan't bother with all that,' said Belle airily.

'You won't get a post.'

'Oh, won't I?' said Belle, and laughed. 'Why should I bother? I'm not going to be a typist all my life.'

'Nor am I,' said Rosa heartily. 'I shall save up for the premium and be a hairdresser.'

'That's not what I meant.' Belle looked down at Rosa as if she were amused. 'One of these days, Rosa, you will hear of me. Everyone will. Belle Lemarchant, it isn't a bad name for a famous person, is it? Would it surprise you, Rosa, if I were to be famous one of these days?'

Rosa felt that nothing Belle did could surprise her. Lately she had been most mysterious. That evening dress! Belle had a new evening dress and it came from Cora Jones, for it had her label inside. It had always been their ambition to have their hats from Wall's and their dresses from Cora Jones, even her advertisements were thrilling.

Love and Romance.
Glorious Bridal Gowns just received from Hollywood
with halo, veil and slip, a gift to every Lucky Bride.

Over and over again they had chosen the dresses they might have, and now Belle had one. She said Miriam had given it to her, but Rosa knew that was not true, for though Miriam would give away her last sweet or pencil at school, she had nothing else to give. The Ramberts were poor and the brothers had no work.

Belle went out to parties with Miriam and strange men; some of them rang her up on the telephone, and she had trained Bruce deSouza to run down and tell her that Miriam wanted to speak to her; they asked her to meet them. How did they know that Belle was old enough and ready to go out? thought Rosa. How did they know?

Rosa's blood ran high and her heart beat, but still she was left in the garden with only Robert. When Robert held her and kissed her she felt as cool and detached as a cloud; watching the shape of his ear against the sky, she wondered if she were really in love.

'You'll come to-morrow?' he whispered. 'Earlier than to-night?'

She turned her cheek on his shoulder to hide a little yawn.

Belle went to Lepri's restaurant and brought back a fancy hat made as well as a real one, and a grey velvet hippopotamus with pink feet.

'What nonsense,' cried auntie. 'How can people go there to be given such childish things?'

'It was a gala night,' boasted Bella. 'It cost twelve rupees for each person's dinner.'

'Twelve rupees!' screeched auntie, and then was silent as she tried to calculate how many dinners she could have given for that.

Against this glamour Robert gave Rosa a paper of carnations and a pair of gloves.

'Why gloves?' asked Rosa.

'I have never seen someone wear gloves,' explained Robert shyly. 'Even if you don't wear them I should like to think you had them.'

Robert was too reverent and too gentle; he kissed her as if she were precious and holy, not at all as she wanted to be kissed. She wanted someone easy and gay, she wanted to dance and have an evening dress and be given at least cigarettes and scent, not gloves and flowers.

'Oh, I feel so dull,' she yawned in Robert's face, like a little cat. 'I think I shall go out with Belle.'

Robert did not take fire. 'Go if you want to,' he said, but she could not bring herself to go. Rosa imagined the men that Belle went out with as mysterious and sinister, wine-dark, with shirt-fronts glossy as white paint, and hands accustomed to handle nothing less expensive than champagne glasses and cigarettes, banknotes and women. She had been told about those men, men of a different social world from hers, and she had heard of the girls who went with them. Suddenly she clung to Robert.

'Robert, Robert,' she whispered, 'I do love you, I do,' and for the first time Robert kissed her as if he would draw her heart through her lips. Rosa twisted herself away.

'Don't, don't!' she cried, 'you mustn't kiss me like that.'

'I can't help it. I love you. Why not, Rosa, why not?'

'Supposing our fathers found out?'

'They can't do anything to us. We'll be married soon.'

But the words were empty and Rosa sighed. 'I wish we could be.'

How could they be married when they had no money and Robert could not get work? There was nothing he could do. His father would not train him for anything. He said it was a waste of time, except to keep him out of mischief, and there was no money for that. It was true, even the trained men could not get work.

'Now we have a typewriter,' Rosa sighed again, 'and I shall have to work in an office. I don't want to work in an office.'

'I won't let you,' said Robert firmly. 'I won't have you in an office. We shall be married.'

'Yes,' said Rosa, but neither of them believed it.

That morning the typewriter and the crowded room made Rosa despair. Auntie was cooking, and curry smells came from the pantry where Boy banged pans and swished water as they worked. Father was resting on his bed with all his clothes on, and Belle, like a thorn-prick to Rosa, in her white skirt and handkerchief top, was polishing her nails on the veranda. It was Rosa's turn at the typewriter; she had not done her hair and she was still in her kimono.

She looked discontentedly round the room. The distemper had mildewed on the walls and a leg had come off the couch, which Boy had propped up with a brick. There was another brick to hold open the partition door into the bedroom. There was wire-netting over the windows to keep out thieves, and it was rusty and sagging. Even the plating was worn on the cruet and épergne that stood on the sideboard, so that they showed stains of yellow; between them was Blanche's goldfish bowl, where Edward her goldfish lived beside a dish of fruit. Someone had left the skins of the eaten fruit on the dish so that the room reeked of bananas. It was auntie's habit to leave the cloth on the table because the wood was marked from hot plates: after the first meal it was usually soiled, especially where father sat. In the cracks of the basket chairs dust had collected, no scrubbing could get it out; and the curtains that shut off the pantry and windows did not match. The bedroom was no better. Auntie, Belle, Rosa and Blanche slept there, and there was hardly room to move between the beds; auntie had taken up the only space, a niche in the wall, to make a recess for her Image and her lamp. The girls were always falling over her *prie-dieu*.

There was a bowl of late sweet peas by Rosa's elbow as she worked, red and pink scented flowers that glowed in the room, but they only made her crosser. Belle had put them there because she had too many for her table; she came and leant over Rosa's shoulder and tapped out the alphabet. Her nails smelt of pear-drops.

'Go away,' said cross Rosa, 'and I wish you would move your flowers. They're in my way.'

'Don't you like them?' cried Belle gaily. 'I put them there for you.' She picked out a flower and twirled it on her fingers. When she said 'you' her mouth was a kiss, a mocking O.

'Your skirt is too tight,' said Rosa spitefully, and went to the veranda and leaned over the railing. But the garden was untidy, the flowers beginning to seed, and there was a congregation of crows worshipping a dead rat they had dropped on the grass.

'It is those filthy deSouzas,' cried Rosa, and set her teeth. 'They throw out their rubbish so carelessly.' Belle would have sent for the sweeper to take it away or even gone herself and thrown it into the refuse tin, but Rosa lamented and mooned back to the typewriter and sat down, looking hopelessly at it with her cheek on her hand.

'What a fuss you make over things,' said Belle. 'No wonder you've no time for anything. You'll never get on.'

'*You* only get on because you don't care what you do.'

'Why should I care?' asked Belle, lighting a cigarette from a packet of 'Goldflake'. 'It doesn't matter what I do. Who am I? No one. Who cares about me? No one. Who knows about me? No one.'

'All of Calcutta must know about you by now, the way you've been behaving.'

'All of Calcutta,' jeered Belle. 'We know a handful of people in Calcutta and most of them are nobodies too. What is Calcutta? It's not the world.'

'It's where we live.'

'I shan't live here very long.' Belle stretched her arms and yawned. 'And get this in your head, Rosa; it doesn't matter what we do because we have nothing to lose. If you are wise you'll do anything to get you on, anything for money, anything to get you away from here. If you don't help yourself no one will help you. I tell you this, and you know it's true. We come from nowhere ...'

'Father says that we are an old family.'

'And auntie says we have bad blood. Perhaps they're both right. We shall never know, and still we are nothing and nobodies.'

'You say that because we're Anglo-Indians,' said Rosa bitterly.

'No, I do *not*,' answered Belle. 'Look at old Barton. He is an Anglo-Indian, but he can trace his family back and back without an atom of dark blood, all decent and respectable people. He has a right to be proud, he has something to be proud of, and what have we? Father says we are an old family. Can we ever believe what father says? Why, auntie tells us that we were called Marchant until he said he was French and put on the Le! No, thank you. I know what I am, at any rate, and it's a pity you don't!' Blowing rings of smoke, Belle went to the sideboard to look at herself in the mirror, bending down to curl her hair with her finger. 'At any rate he has given me nice ears.'

'Who has?'

'Father. Oh, Rosa! The fish, Blanche's goldfish; he's dead.'

'Edward? He's not!' cried Rosa, springing up to see.

'He must be. He's floating.' Belle picked his body out of the water. 'Ouch! he's gone all flabby.'

'Put him back!' screamed Rosa. 'Oh, I can't bear anything dead. Oh, my God, put him back, Belle. What will Blanche say?'

'Why didn't you have the vet?' said Blanche when she came in, her eyes black with anger. 'Couldn't you see he was sick?'

'I'll buy you another, darling,' Rosa consoled her. 'They are only two annas. I'll buy another fish.'

'You have terrible ideas,' said Blanche coldly. 'I shall never have another. I don't want another. What an awful thing to think of.'

Rosa was hurt, her easy tears filled her eyes. Blanche looked at her with a stiff face; she had seen Rosa cry too often to be moved by it, but she said kindly, 'Don't cry, Rosa, you needn't cry for Edward. He wasn't *your* fish.'

'It isn't only Edward; it's the day,' sniffed Rosa.

'Yes. It has been a bad day,' said Blanche.

Every day she hated going to school where, because they had no money and auntie was so pious, she was taken for nothing, and everyone knew it; the girls and the teachers, the teaching nuns and the nuns who did not teach, and the convent servants, and the house servants who came to fetch away the girls, all knew that Blanche Lemarchant was taken for nothing, and auntie sent her breakfast down in a cake-tin with a cloth tied over it instead of a proper aluminium carrier like the others.

'Why was the day bad?' asked Rosa.

Something awful had happened. On the way to school Blanche had met Maureen and Wendy Fernandes and their mother. Their mother had a purple parasol, and they all had rings in their ears, and their ayah came behind them carrying their things; Blanche shrank against the wall hiding her case.

'Hullo, Blanche Lemarchant,' said Wendy.

'Who is this child?' demanded Mrs Fernandes. 'Who is she?'

Wendy looked at her feet and mumbled.

'Who is she? I want to know.'

'I only wished her, mumma,' said Wendy. 'I had to wish her.'

'You know,' said Mrs Fernandes, 'that I am very particular. You know I do not let you speak to children in the street. You know that, ayah, and this child is dark; she's nearly black.'

'I'm not,' said Blanche in a cold, dignified voice, that came far up above the burning place that Mrs Fernandes's words seemed to have made inside her, 'I am only a very pale brown.' But Mrs Fernandes had tittupped away down the street.

Blanche was not going to tell Rosa that, and she said, 'All the time at school I was hungry.'

'Hungry? Had you no breakfast?'

'Boy is so slow that sometimes he doesn't get there until after recreation is over.'

'Why didn't you ask Mother Ignatius?'

'I wouldn't ask Mother Ignatius for anything,' said Blanche stoutly. 'And I got a bad mark for my blouse again. It splits at the back and that isn't my fault, is it, because I can't see behind my shoulders? It is one of yours, and you sweated so under your arms that auntie had to take out the sleeves and put them in again. That is why it is so narrow, but I can't tell them that, can I?'

She was silent, staring at Edward as he floated on the water on his side.

Once there had been a cat that came into the garden and lay on the creepers in the sun, but father would not let her give it milk, and presently it went away. Then she pretended she had a puppy called Fox, but she knew he could never be real.

'How should I pay to feed a puppy?' asked father. 'It's bad enough to have to feed you.'

That could not cost him much because often she did not eat what there was, and the cat might just as well have had her milk.

Then at Christmas Rosa gave her a bowl and she bought Edward. She had chosen him from a tub full of fishes in the market, and he had not cost father an anna because the babu clerk at the china stall where they sold live fish was her friend and gave her puffed rice for nothing. Edward's double-finned tail had waved in the water, his fairy colours flickered behind his green glass walls, his mouth opened and shut like a purse when he came up for his grains of rice, and now he was dead. Blanche had a hard tight feeling in her throat. But she could not cry, though the tears were burning her eyes.

'I'll take him into the pantry,' she said calmly. 'Boy will help me to bury him.'

Later that evening she said: 'I saw a little dog on the stairs, Rosa; it wasn't like Fox, although it was white too, you know. It was small and silky and it had ears like a spaniel, all curly, and it had goggle eyes like a peke.'

'What could it have been?' said Rosa.

'I don't know what it was, but someone called it "Echo! Echo!" like that. Wasn't that a funny name for a dog?'

'What things you think of!'

'She called him that. I didn't think of it,' said Blanche, but afterwards she wondered if she had.

Never before had there been a little dog called Echo on the stairs.

# 4

The deSouzas were very good-natured over lending the use of the telephone, which was in their private flat. They were ready to share anything. Blanche said they shared a tooth-brush.

'How *filthee!*' cried Rosa. 'Don't you, Blanche, play with them any more.'

Auntie was silent, for she was not going to tell them that she had not seen a tooth-brush until she went to board at school; the children, she and her brothers and sisters, had used twigs split at the ends into a brush. The juice kept their teeth white, and surely that was clean, for they had always thrown the twigs away.

Blanche did not care if the deSouzas were clean or not; she liked them and had even had a turn at the tooth-brush. Now she came and told Belle that Eileen deSouza had run down to tell her she was wanted on the telephone.

'All that way up. Oh, my God!' grumbled Belle to Rosa, who would have flown to answer it if the telephone had rung for her.

'It's a party,' she called as she came back. 'I said I'd take you, Rosa. They want another girl.'

'Take *me*? But Robert—'

'Now listen to me,' said Belle, putting her hands on her hips and facing Rosa, 'now listen, Rosa. Are you going to be stupid all your life? This is the last time I'll ask you, and it is the last time I'll bother if you are.'

Rosa went to the party in Belle's old white dress with the top cut off and a bodice made of black velvet marguerites, that met across the shoulders with strappings of ciré ribbon.

The tailor brought it at the last minute, and when Rosa had it on, he put in the last stitches with a needle and thread that he took from his thimble-shaped hat. She felt sick. She was burning hot and cold by turns, and her hands shook so that she could hardly dress. Twice she put down her things to tell Belle that really she could not go, but each time she dared not say it. The bodice of marguerites was low and tight, the ribbon that held it up narrow and frail; Rosa was worried.

'How shall I wear my vest?' she asked.

'Don't be silly. How can you wear a vest? You can't.'

'You'll have nothing but your knickers on, then,' said Blanche.

'Well, what more does she want?'

Blanche slapped a mosquito on her leg and Belle looked up and said, 'Go and get a glass of water.' She always spoke to Blanche as if she were an idiot or a servant. 'Get a glass of water, and must you make that noise with your shoes?'

'I must, because they're too big and too high,' Blanche answered sadly, and indeed they were an old pair of Rosa's, velvet and very shoddy.

'Have you no shoes of your own?'

'No, except my school shoes. But I shall have,' she added more happily, 'when we have the money auntie will fetch them from the Chinaman, they went to be mended and he won't give them back until we pay. I wish he would,' she sighed. 'These are very uncomfortable and they smell.'

'Go and get that water,' said Belle unsympathetically. 'Rosa, you can't wear those knickers.'

'Why can't I? They've got lace on.'

Belle was not listening. 'Oh, I *wish* I had some stockings,' she said.

'Stockings!' cried Rosa. 'We have never worn stockings, and if we did they wouldn't show, but I show through this dress, Belle. I wish I could wear my vest. I look a sight.'

But when she followed Belle into William's drawing-room all the heads turned towards them like flowers towards the sun. The eyes of the men rested on them, but the girls' eyes glanced from head to heel and turned back to the men; only in their smiles which grew a little harder, and their voices, raised and more emphatic, and the way they arched their necks and defiantly drank their cocktails, they showed that they were aware of Belle and Rosa. They were showing a yellow light that might change to red or green.

Belle went straight across to them. She had a string of young men behind her, but she talked only to the man who had brought them to the party.

'Mr Harman, my sister Rosa.'

He had squeezed her hand and looked into her eyes until Belle said, '*Do* come along! We shall be late.'

Rosa had sat at the back of the car, now she sat at the back of the party; someone had given her a drink, white and cloudy like the sal volatile auntie gave them for headaches, and it had a bitter taste like medicine. The room was full of girls sitting demurely together and noisy young men in white dinner jackets.

Some of the girls were very dark, and Belle was by far the prettiest. She was still talking to Mr Harman and, looking at him, Rosa thought how thick he was; his fingers and his wrists, his neck above his solid body, even his trousers seemed too well filled; there was something overpowering about those thick white legs that shocked Rosa. She did not like Mr Harman. His hair was curious, like black wire growing far back on his forehead, so that he had an immensely high face and eyebrows like the clowns she had seen when Hagenbeck's Circus came to Calcutta. He was fascinated by Belle; he could not stop touching her, her hand, her shoulder, even fingering her dress or her bag. His hands were covered with the same upstanding hair. Rosa shuddered; she could not bear to see them touching Belle.

Belle was quite rude to him, contradicting him, answering him back, but he seemed enchanted, and presently the young men fell away, and they were left alone; Rosa went and stood beside Belle.

'Don't follow me about,' said Belle, without turning her head. 'Don't cling on to me.' She gave Rosa a little push. 'You'll have to find someone else to take you home.'

'But I don't *know* anyone—' began Rosa urgently. Belle walked off and left her standing there.

She felt as stiff and as large as an advertisement figure cut out of cardboard with all the lights beating down upon her. She twitched her dress straight and sipped her unpleasant-tasting drink.

'Where *is* William?' cried a girl, tall and elegant, with tortoise-shell ear-rings. 'Isn't this his party?'

'He gives so many parties,' said a young man gravely, 'you can't expect him to go to them all.'

He was a very young man with yellow hair and a face suntanned like a girl's. Presently he came and asked Rosa to dance.

As they danced he asked her: 'What's your name? Mine's Stephen, Stephen Bright. I'm William's cousin.'

'Oh!' said Rosa, who had no idea who William was. 'I'm Rosa Lemarchant.'

'Are you French?'

'No.' She hesitated. 'I'm European.'

Stephen had been in India one day when he met Rosa. All his life, if there was a thing he had sworn he would not do, it was to go into business, which was precisely what he had done now. He had been unsatisfactory at school, labelled 'not dependable' in his reports, and too satisfactory at home, where his mother and old nannie adored him; he had wanted to be an actor, a film actor, a choreographer, and a journalist, and asked his father to think it over. His father thought it over and sent him out to India; but Stephen had seen Uday Shankar dance in London and was reconciled.

He read every book he could find on India, steeped himself indiscriminately in its poetry and history, and was overcome with excitement when he learnt that his great-uncle Howard had been in the East India Company.

Already he had walked round the Fort and along the Strand Road by the Hooghli where the water was cloudy, the colour of lemon squash, and like wicker beetles the country boats crawled from side to side, among the B.I. boats, Japanese and German tramps and paddle-wheel river steamers. He had astounded his cousin William by asking what the monuments were.

'What monuments?' asked William, who knew the Cenotaph because of Armistice Day and the Victoria Memorial because it was too big to miss.

As soon as he saw Stephen, William knew that he must be

altered at once, without delay, before he became public. Already he had told him not to say divine, asked him to take down his Gaudier-Brzeska 'sleeping doe' and sent away his bearer.

Stephen had engaged the bearer in Bombay, he was paid and spoke English like a duke, and in his place came a Lepcha with bow-legs and a face like a Chinese.

'How can I speak to him?' complained Stephen.

'You'll learn,' said William. 'And can't you wear a topee, Stephen, instead of that horrible hat? Why didn't you get one at Simon Artz?'

That hurt Stephen, who had taken such particular pains not to get a topee at Simon Artz.

But William was also kind. He met Stephen at Howrah Station, and brought him back to the house and introduced him to Gray, who lived with him, took him down to the office and introduced him again to Sir Thomas Rallings, his chief, gave him lunch at Lepri's and asked him to his party. 'It's a B party,' he said.

'What's a B party?'

'A and B. B girls.'

'Oh, I see,' said Stephen, and began to wonder about these Eurasian girls of whom he had heard so much, who were so alluring and so dangerous.

'What happens?' he asked.

'Usual thing,' said William. 'They behave very well and we behave very badly, and then they behave worse.'

'Oh!' said Stephen again. 'Do you think, William, that you would mind if I bought some curtains for my bedroom? I mean it's rather like a boot-box now, isn't it? Thin tomato-coloured ones would be rather perfect, wouldn't they?'

'Delicious,' said William sourly.

When Stephen asked Rosa to dance she was as dazzled as if she had been caught up to heaven in a chariot of fire, and if his arms had been God's chariot they could not have felt more wonderful to her. She had a tremor like hiccups in her breath and her knees were stiff with trying to dance too well. Stephen seemed to want to dance with her all evening, so that she could not have been very bad. As if in a dream she took in the rooms, larger than all their three put together, they seemed spacious and empty to Rosa even with the crowd of people, for the rooms she knew were always over-full. She thought it an enormous flat for just three people, Stephen and the William they talked about, and Mr Gray.

'Do you sleep here alone?' she asked Stephen, in spite of Belle's frown, when he took them into his room to powder their noses.

'Yes,' said Stephen, amused. 'I couldn't bear to share a room.'

'It would be hateful. I couldn't bear it either,' said Belle, and Rosa opened her eyes wide, for she thought she was the one in the family who told lies.

She was very surprised to see that the bed was an ordinary iron one such as she slept on herself, and when she sat down on the couch the springs had gone. But Stephen was not in the least abashed; and for supper they stood about or sat on the floor with plates of sausages and scrambled eggs that she called rumble-tumble, or kippers, with great hunks of bread. Stephen drank beer, not champagne, as she had imagined he would. Yet these were the people who belonged to clubs and went to Government House, whose doings were reported in the papers.

Now the party had broken up into couples who drifted away.

'What time is it?' asked Rosa.

'Quite early, only three.'

'Onlee three!' She could not believe it had gone so quickly. 'I must go home. Has – has Belle gone?'

'I think she has,' said Stephen evasively. 'I'll take you home. Come and find William and I'll take you home.'

William was lying on a couch with his shoes off, large and plump with a red face and red hair, and the girl with the tortoise-shell ear-rings was sitting on a cushion by his side. They were eating an ice off the same plate, feeding each other with their spoons.

'Go away, we're being vicious,' he said when he saw Stephen, and 'Hallo, darling, do you love me?' to Rosa.

'William, can I borrow your car?'

'Whaffor?'

'To take Rosa home.'

'She can't go home. It's not time. She doesn't want to go home, do you, darling?'

'Let her go home if she wants,' said the tortoise-shell girl.

Rosa had been dancing all evening with Stephen; her cheeks were hot, the ciré ribbon stuck to her shoulders, and her breasts, the nipples showing through her dress, rose up and down as she breathed. She smiled happily at William.

'Can I have your car?' repeated Stephen.

'No, you can't,' said William. 'If she wants to go, I'll take her home myself.'

The tortoise-shell girl looked sulky and William laughed.

'We'll get a taxi,' said Stephen to Rosa.

'Now he's cross!' complained William. 'Don't be cross, little cousin Stephen. You can have my car. I'll give it you. It's outside at the gate.'

'William's a fatuous fool!' said Stephen.

'I rather liked him,' said Rosa.

They drove down the Lower Circular Road to the race-course. 'Show me the way to the river,' he said.

The railings of the race-course glittered with dew under the street lamps, but the spaces of the maidan were dense and dark as velvet; only the sky was curiously light, with stars as big as sequins of Indian gold.

'You would never see a sky like that in England,' said Stephen. 'It's magnificent. But it wants drums and barbaric colours and a shuttered wall and a dancing girl with bare brown breasts—'

'What is the sky like in England?' asked Rosa quickly.

They drove through Hastings and along by the river where the wind came off the water and cooled their cheeks and chilled Rosa's shoulders; she had no coat, the family had only two coats, a blazer and auntie's black corded silk that she had from Mr Kempf, and neither of them would do for a party. They never had coats or shoes or warm vests for the winter, but they had plenty of voiles and silk frocks and diamante bands and clips. She shivered as they turned into the Red Road.

'This part of Calcutta fascinates me,' said Stephen. 'I like to think of the people who lived in these old streets. Philip Francis, the lovely Madame Grand, Marion Hastings – all of them. I like to think they are driving here still in their phaetons and curricles and that we are driving with them. And perhaps if we could see further there would be other, stranger people, the people of the future.'

Rosa laughed, and Stephen said earnestly, 'Don't you believe it? Quite a lot of people do.'

'I don't understand,' said Rosa. 'How could we see the future or the past?'

'Suppose,' said Stephen, 'suppose time was a road that we were walking along; behind us, round a bend, is an inn, and now we are on a bridge, and round the next corner is a clump of trees; the inn is past for us, the bridge is present and the clump of trees to come is our future. Yet when I describe them I say "is an inn", "is a bridge", "is a clump of trees", because they are all there together. To anyone up above, they are seen all in one, past, present and future co-existent.'

'Yes, if we had wings.'

'And haven't we wings?' cried Stephen. 'Haven't we wings?'

'We live in a house that is supposed to be haunted,' offered Rosa, and she looked at Stephen's attractive face and wished he would not talk so much.

In Chowringhee, Lepri's was closed, but there were still boys running after the cars with balloons and carnations and magazines to sell.

Rosa showed Stephen a turning into a street that belonged to all time, narrow and twisting with the shuttered houses of a midnight Spain, and presently she stopped him at a double gate that had a door let into it.

'This is our place,' she said, giving him her hand to say good night. But he was staring up at the house.

'Let me look,' he said. 'I've never seen an old house in India. It is old, isn't it? Can I come in? You use the little door, don't you?'

There was light enough from the stars to see the high front with its window-shutters open to catch the breeze; to see the pattern the cassia trees made above the drive, like lace against the sky, and the colonnades of the porch.

'It's *huge*,' he whispered. 'Do you live in all?'

'No-o,' said Rosa reluctantly, 'our suite is at the side,' and she showed him the path to the garden under their windows. The wind moved the palm-leaves and from far away came the sound of drums.

'Are the windows arched? And the roof? I can't quite see, but it looks like a chapel.'

A car passed down the side street; its headlights fell on the palms, across the lawn and on the windows.

'What is that on the windows?' cried Stephen, 'and what's that on the lawn? I say, this is interesting! Is that something carved over the windows?'

'It's carving in plaster.'

'You can't carve plaster,' said Stephen quickly. 'You mean it's a cast or a modelling?'

'Well, I don't know,' said Rosa, 'but it's a flower and an animal with a sword or a spear in its head.'

'You mean in its heart.'

'No, in its head.'

'That's curious. Very odd, and on the lawn, what is that? It looks like a stump with creepers on it.'

'It is,' said Rosa. 'It's covered with jasmine.'

'And underneath?'

'We don't know. Probably it is rubbish.'

'But haven't you looked? Do you mean you haven't *looked*?'

'It is unlucky to break jasmine,' said Rosa; 'it brings sorrow. Don't you know you must never break jasmine?'

She spoke so earnestly that Stephen turned and looked at her. Her dress glimmered in the darkness and as she walked in front of him to the porch it seemed to fall and spread like a waterfall. They went into the porch where the steps led up to the empty vestibule.

'You give me a strange feeling,' said Stephen, 'as if you were taking me to another world. I've been on the edge of mine, I have only to step out of it into yours. I'm not even sure which world you belong to, Rosa.'

The shadow of a pillar was thrown faintly by the starlight across her dress, like the ribbon of an order bestowed on a foreign lady.

'Have you ever been in love?' Stephen asked her.

'N-no,' said Rosa, 'have you?'

'Often, and I think I'm doing it again – or am I? Perhaps it's just your strangeness and your house. I love your house, Rosa. Can I come and see it to-morrow in the daylight?'

'If you like,' said Rosa crossly. Perhaps it was just 'your house' that rankled.

'You said that as if you didn't want me.'

Rosa hesitated. If Blanche could be sent away to play and father went out and auntie kept on her shoes – she sighed; there were so many things that Stephen would still notice and she would be ashamed.

'You could look at it from the garden,' she said. 'We wouldn't worry you at all and Mr deSouza wouldn't mind.'

Before her eyes Stephen turned into a sulky child. He kicked the step like any baby and said, 'But I want to see *you*.'

Rosa's knees went weak with wonder, her heart seemed to melt into her stomach. 'Come to-morrow,' she whispered. 'Come to-morrow.'

She would have lifted the arch of heaven and let him in, but he only said, 'At six, then?' and shook her hand and went away.

# 5

'So you didn't enjoy your party,' said Robert.

'But I did,' said Rosa. 'I did. I enjoyed it very much.'

'Then why were you crying?'

'*Crying?* Why should I cry?'

'I saw you, as a matter of fact,' said Robert. 'I waited for you to come in. I waited on the stairs, and you were so late that I must have fallen asleep. Then I woke up and saw you crying. I was coming to speak to you when you ran away into your room. First I heard the gharry drive away—'

'Gharry!' cried Rosa in scorn. 'I came home in a car. A gentleman, why shouldn't I tell you, his name is Mr Bright, he brought me home in his car and we talked a little; he was interested in the house, and then he went away and I came inside.'

'I don't know about the gentleman, but you were crying. You leant against that pillar and hid your face, and as soon as I came up to you, you ran away. Why did you do that, Rosa?'

'You saw someone else.'

'Don't tell lies,' said Robert sternly, and Rosa opened her eyes wide in surprise. 'Do you think I don't know you? It was quite light and I saw your blue dress.'

'Blue! My dress was not blue. It was white. Now will you believe me?'

'It was blue,' insisted Robert, and he blushed. 'And, Rosa, the front was too low. I don't like you to wear disgusting dresses like that.'

'Really!' mocked Rosa. 'I shall wear what dresses I choose, Robert deSouza, and what I choose could never be disgusting. I suppose Belle was there too, and what had she on that you did not like?'

'I don't remember seeing Belle,' said Robert slowly. 'And yet I could say she was there too, but there was only one of you,' he added, puzzled, 'in a deep-blue dress, rather the colour of those morning-glory flowers.'

'It shows how foolish you are, Bob,' said Rosa more gently. 'My dress was white and, even without my vest, it wasn't indecent. You've been dreaming.'

But Robert remembered clearly, how in his sleep he had seemed to hear music, and then he had been troubled by the people passing and repassing him on the stairs, a nightmare feeling of bumping and jostling that had woken him; as he started up, still in his sleep, he thought someone paused on the step beside him, and the jealousy he had felt for Rosa turned suddenly to an anguished grief, and he had hung there on the stair rail fixed in his misery; then he heard weeping and had gone to find Rosa, but she ran away.

'Why did you do that?' he said. 'Why were you so unkind? Why did you run away and why do you lie to me?'

'And why did you spy on me? What business is it of yours where I go or what I do?'

'Rosa, don't talk to me like that,' pleaded Robert. 'Isn't it my business what you do? Every little thing you do I care for.'

'Well, I wish you wouldn't. I don't belong to you and I wish you would remember that.'

'Very well, I shan't care,' said Robert. 'Go where you like and do what you like and be what you like. Go for a whore like your sister Belle, for all I care.'

'Robert!' cried Rosa; her hands flew up to her face and suddenly she began to cry. 'Oh! Don't say that, Bob! Bob! I can't bear to think of Belle.'

Belle had come in when it was light, when the birds were waking in the stillness that comes just before the morning. She woke Rosa by blundering into her bed; she moved about the room like a poor blind moth that had lost its wings. Her face was sick and livid, her shoulders dirty, her hair was full of leaves; and the dress, the lovely dress was torn and stained, the bodice split open, one strap broken so that she had to hold it up round her.

'Belle!' breathed Rosa in a frightened whisper. 'Belle!'

She was struggling out of her dress, and looked up quickly at Rosa's whisper.

'Hush! can't you?' she hissed, shivering. 'Hush or you'll wake them.'

'Oh, Belle! What did he do to you?'

'The brute. The dirty beast,' whispered Belle, shivering violently. 'He took me out to Barrackpore and wouldn't come back. He pulled me out of the car, he rolled me on the grass. Look, he's bitten me.' But Rosa had hidden her face in the bed-clothes. She saw those thick hairy fingers like a spider on Belle's body, fastening on her, creeping down her bodice.

'Oh-h,' she moaned.

'Shut up! Do you want to wake auntie?' Belle kicked the dress under the cupboard and looked under her pillow for her night-gown. 'I'll teach him to do that to me,' she said.

Rosa sat up. 'Belle, you're not going with him after *this?*'

She had said that again next evening, when Belle came through the sitting-room with her bag and her new white dress on.

'You're not going out with him *again?*'

'Don't be more of a fool than you can help,' said Belle coldly. 'This is just when I *am* going out with him.'

Now Rosa, talking to Robert, was filled with hot rage against all of them, against Belle's Mr Harman and Stephen and the strange friends she had wanted, and against Robert himself. She looked at Robert with such hatred that he said, 'I'm sorry, Rosa, I didn't mean to say that. You would never be like Belle, but you know what happens when girls like – you and Belle and my sisters go out with men in – society whose names you read in the paper. I am sorry I said that, and you may think I was spying on you, but I did see you crying and I wish you would tell me why.'

'I was not crying,' said Rosa. 'I don't believe you saw me. You are trying to find out what I did because you're jealous. I don't believe you saw anyone.'

And on her words, above their heads a voice floated down the wall of the stairs, a voice that was like Rosa's or Belle's, a young girl's voice.

'Echo! Echo!' it called.

# 6

When Stephen woke next morning he lay in bed thinking of Rosa and her home with the pillars and the whispering palms.

Outside it was already dusty and still, the bougainvillia he could see from his window burned against a white sky, his pyjamas felt sticky and his sheets were warm to touch. Even on the hottest days in summer at home he did not remember waking to this dry, excited air, and instead of the summer birds that filled the garden at Tigley Cross here were only the one-note crows, sounding over and over again from the mango tree.

He had been born and brought up at Tigley Cross, in one of those grey Devonshire houses shaped like a bad L, where the kitchens and backyards seem twice as large as the house. He had been brought up by nannie with selected hours with his mother and occasional whippings from his father.

Stephen was one of the few people who are saved by being spoilt. Had nannie been a disciplinarian, his mother more domineering, his father less lazy or himself less good at games, he might have grown up sulky and repressed; he was an embryo rebel who had nothing to rebel against; and as a result he may have been thoughtless and graceless, but he was quite charming.

He had gone to school and done exactly the same as everyone else of his age and class; been to the same sort of places, kept the same sort of animals, worn the same sort of clothes and, his father said, talked rather more nonsense but the same kind of nonsense.

This new life was as different as Rosa was different from the girls he had known at home. He lay and thought about her; her skin was like paper, matt white, her body flimsy, and he remembered her lips that were dark, dark red. Yet she reminded him of his little sister Janet; that was why he had not kissed her last night, although he knew she had expected him to.

Once they had taken Janet to the *Tosca* of a touring opera company at Totnes, and Tosca had been a giantess with short arms and Scarpio a Glaxo baby; Stephen remembered how they had chased each other round and round the sofa, while the floorboards shook, and Scarpio had died neatly on the carpet, lifting his legs out of the draughts at the last moment, and how he and his mother had laughed. Janet turned round and rebuked them; he had suddenly seen it with Janet's eyes as beautiful, tragic, dramatic, and ceased to laugh.

With a feeling beyond his years and his usual self, he sensed that Rosa was like that, too; naïve and utterly serious, and in his feeling for her was a pity and a tenderness as for something precious; and because of her strangeness and the strangeness of the house she lived in, there was a piquancy mingled with it that excited him.

In his mind he turned again off Chowringhee into that street, narrow and winding past the yellow-plastered houses, and came to the gate with the leading door and saw the milky pillars and the palms above the lawn.

'I'm going there to-day,' said Stephen. 'I'm going to look under that creeper, perhaps I shall find something rare.' And he smiled as he remembered how Rosa had said that it was unlucky to break the jasmine.

How absurd and ridiculous she is, he thought, and wondered what William would say.

William's bearer was squeezing a sponge high above his head trying to wake him. But William slept on, his mouth slightly open; he still had his evening shirt and socks on, and Stephen went thoughtfully away.

After office he drove in a taxi across the maidan to Chowringhee. The roads were streaming with cars, all coming from the direction of Clive Street and the offices, and the mounted policemen, in magnificent white with scarlet turbans, rode watchfully along the grass verges.

On the stretches of grass hundreds of children were playing round their gabbling ayahs, and less fortunate than the children, who were at any rate allowed to run free, hundreds of dogs drooped at the end of their chains, trailed to the nearest piece of grass to sit captive, while their sweepers sat in a circle and gossiped.

Behind the Fort funnels and spars and derricks showed from the ships at anchor in the river, and as they turned left to Chowringhee, from the trees came the circling of crows as they swept up into the sky and settled again for the night.

He found the turning, but now the street was crowded. Children were coming in from play, whole families were driving out packed into one hired victoria, rickshaws edged past in the gutter; dhobies ran past with a dress, starched and ironed, borne on a hanger, and elderly ladies sat out on verandas, fanning themselves and talking across the street.

When Stephen came to the gates and the little door he saw that the house was on the corner of a lane, and that the railings along the wall were broken, with wire-netting put up behind them, and the corner wall had been let as a hoarding. Through the door he looked up at the house.

He had been afraid that by daylight it could not be the same, that the enchantment had been given to the glimmering palm-leaves and the house and the columns by the starlight; but now through the shoddiness and decay he saw it again.

The windows with their slatted shutters along the house wall made mysterious shadows against the yellow plaster; the columns soaring to the porch, the flight of steps, the drive width that was preposterous for its length, were all as he remembered them. He saw the cracks and stains on the walls, the weeds that had pushed up the stones, the fallen plaster, and smelt the smell of drains and rubbish and old damp earth, but there was an ole-ander by the gate with crisp pink flowers and poinsettias with long-fingered scarlet petals round the house.

Among the children playing on the steps was a young man, dark and curly-haired, reading in a basket chair. He went indoors when he saw Stephen and defiantly came back at once and picked up his book, but Stephen knew he was not reading but watching him.

The children stared, and one, a girl, came after him, walking on her toes so that he should not hear her. Her eyes were big as she took him in: his hair, his sun-tan and palm-beach suit, she had never seen anything as beautiful; now that she had seen him, she did not blame Rosa for turning her out of the rooms. When she had seen him in at the front, she went round to the back and stayed there, for she did not want him to notice her on his way out.

Father had been sent out, too; he had been lured to Entally by an advertisement of a Frigidaire for sale: 'Apply between six and seven,' it said, which fitted in well, and Rosa had not told him that the cutting was ten days old. Auntie had to keep her shoes on and wear her dress that the tailor had altered, and Belle had gone out with Mr Harman.

'Why should I want to see your Stephen Bright?' asked Belle. 'Why do you bring him here?'

'He is interested in the house, besides, he's my friend.'

'House!' scoffed Belle. 'And do you think he'll be your friend after he sees where you live? He'll know exactly what you are and what he can do. You are silly, Rosa.'

'You don't understand. He's different.'

'Don't give yourself away to him all the same,' said Belle more kindly than she usually spoke. 'You don't know what he is like and very few of them are different – with us, Rosa.'

Then she had gone out, flippant and calm and smiling. When she thought of that Rosa did not want Stephen to come, she did not want to see him or any man again, not even Robert who was so safe; she wanted to go back to the convent where the only men were Father Ghezzi and the other priests. 'Oh, I hope he doesn't come,' she cried, walking backwards and forwards in front of the windows. 'Perhaps he has forgotten. I'm sure he has forgotten. It's late. He won't come now. Do you think he has forgotten?'

'It's two minutes past six,' said auntie, 'and he said he would come at six.'

When he came, Stephen sat opposite auntie in uncomfortable silence.

'A peg, Mr Bright?' said auntie. 'You will have a peg?' And Boy came in with the whisky on the coupon tray, though he had been told to use the other one, and brought the soda with the ice-bran still sticking to it, and he had a dirty glass-cloth over his shoulder, all of which Rosa felt acutely.

Stephen did not notice, he was watching auntie. As she talked she fanned herself, blowing powder in a dust from her cheeks, which were fat and almost the colour of earth. Her hair, which was grey, she wore in a long bob that was curled and waved in front and hung straight at the back, and she had a muslin dress dotted in black. Her eyes reminded Stephen of a monkey's: bright and uncomprehending, taking him in with a monkey interest and understanding nothing.

'I have brought them up from little mites, Mr Bright. They have done so well at school. Rosa never gave me any trouble but Belle was always very fiery, Mr Bright, and clever, if she had entered for her examination, she would have gained at least eighty-five per cent, and they are so popular. Belle is out now to a party with her friends.'

There was a silence. Auntie fanned the powder off her face, Rosa gazed at Stephen and Stephen crossed one leg over the other, pulled up the crease of his beautiful trousers and put his tie straight. Boy dropped a plate in the pantry with a crash and Stephen said, 'I thought you might have an arched roof in here, Mrs Kemp.'

'Kempf,' corrected auntie. 'My husband was a German from Germany. He took a photograph of the Himalayas that won a medal in an exhibition in Europe.' She pronounced Himalayas with a long second syllable, 'Himarlayas'.

'Mr Bright,' said Rosa hastily, 'is interested in historical things and he says, auntie, that this house is historical.'

'The mouldings and structure of this wing,' explained Stephen, 'make me think it must have been a chapel.'

'Oh, no!' cried auntie, much shocked, 'it could never have been that. Who could have been so irreverent as to partition it off?'

Rosa took Stephen into the garden, and now he saw that the house faced south, with the annex and the garden on the east side, and the garden was an oblong with the lane running along its eastern wall, where a creeper was out in stars of frail purples and mauves in wistaria clusters, and another with dangling keys of pink and scarlet.

'What are those?' asked Stephen, but Rosa did not know. Later William told him they were petria and quisqualis. The jasmine was not in flower, only its dark leaves were thick and heavy over the stump that might have been a broken pillar for there were loose bricks on the grass. Stephen pulled the leaves apart and Rosa cried, 'Don't break it. Please don't break it. It's so unlucky to break it, Mr Bright.'

'But I *must* see,' said Stephen irritably; he twisted the creepers away, and in the centre, under the stems, was a circle of metal, smooth and dark and stained with green; jutting up from its centre was a thin triangle of the same metal, set upright.

'What an *extraordinary* thing!' He knelt down on the grass, feeling under the jasmine for the sides of the pillar, and to Rosa's dismay he tore away the clinging stems.

'Oh, be careful.'

'I *am* being careful. We may want to hide it again. Have you got a hammer?'

'What are you going to do?' wailed Rosa. 'You can't knock it down. Mr deSouza would never allow—'

'I'm going to loosen a brick or two, that's all. Please, Rosa, be a good girl, get me a hammer.'

'I'll ask Boy,' said Rosa, and presently came back with a

hammer that Boy had borrowed from who knows where. With smart taps, Stephen sent dust and twigs flying into the air, he was very skilful and seemed to know exactly where to tap, the bricks came easily away.

'They're not cemented,' he said, 'they've been piled up on each other. Whoever did it, did it very badly. Blast this stuff,' and he wrenched away more of the creeper.

'It will bring us bad luck,' said Rosa. 'They say there is a spirit in the jasmine that sends sorrow to you, and Mr deSouza will not like us breaking this down without asking.'

'I'll defy your spirits,' laughed Stephen, 'and Mr deSouza won't know. I'm only taking down one side and we'll cover it up again; besides, if it is what I think it is, he'll be pleased. I can't imagine who can have had one in India. I wonder if it worked with the tropical sun, and why should they brick it up?'

In the fading light, as the bricks fell away under the creeper, they could see a shape emerging, a stem, swelling out like a vase and narrowing again to support the face of stone; below, hidden in the grass, their fingers found the edge of a plinth under the pedestal.

Holding the jasmine back Stephen dusted it with his handkerchief, brushing off dust, twigs, insects and crumbled brick. 'I say, there's some carving here.' He shouted the words in his excitement. 'And a monogram. Two initials. Look.'

'Ssh. They'll hear us and come out.'

'What are they? A,V and it's a B or an R. The carving's here, round to the side. I must chip a little more. I wish to God it wasn't so dark. Can you hold this torch for me?'

'It's the same as the carving over the windows, isn't it?' said Rosa, peering down into the circle of light. 'I'm sure it is. Isn't that the shield and those the crescent moons?'

'Damn, it's half obliterated. Is that an animal, do you suppose? It's chipped just by its head, it's difficult to see.'

'It looks like a horse,' said Rosa doubtfully.

'I never heard of anyone having a horse as their crest,' said Stephen. 'It can't be a horse.'

'It might be a zebra or a donkey,' suggested Rosa.

'Don't joke,' snapped Stephen. 'This is important.'

'I wasn't joking,' said Rosa, surprised. 'And you haven't told me yet what you think it is.'

He stood up and dusted his hands and took the torch from her and studied the circle of metal.

'Here's a name, cut into it. Right on the edge. Look. D-U-V-A-L. Duval. B-O-R-D-E-A-U-X. Bordeaux. 1790.'

'Is that who it belonged to?'

'No, I think it's the maker, there's no "d" in the monogram. They must have brought it out ready cast. It couldn't have worked with the difference in latitude. I wonder why they brought it. Perhaps they had it especially cast, the style is in one piece with the dial. But why did they cover it up?'

'But what *is* it? What do you think it is?'

'It's a sundial,' said Stephen slowly.

'A sundial? What is a sundial?'

'Good Lord, don't you know? No, I suppose you wouldn't. It's a sun clock. You tell the time by the shade of the style, that little arm, thrown by the sun. They go back to the Egyptians. Do you see, here are the markings of the hours, these grooves, they're nearly worn away. God! Here's an inscription. Look, Rosa, look!'

An oblong of marble, no bigger than a card, written in gold, was sunk into the face; the gilt had worn off the lettering but they followed the faint lines.

'Oh,' breathed Stephen, reading it, Rosa's head beside his.

'I can't understand what it says,' said Rosa. 'Is it a foreign language?'

'It's French.' He pored over the writing. '*Mon – seul – dé – sir. Mon seul désir*. Now where have I heard that before?'

'What does it *mean*?' cried Rosa in a loud, imperious voice, and stamped her foot.

Stephen let the jasmine fall, he was suddenly conscious of her there beside him in her starched dress, of the clink of her bangles and the smell of eau-de-Cologne. The garden was empty, the wind that came with the darkness lifted his hair and blew in her dress and the stiff palm-leaves.

'It means – "My only desire, my chief desire."'

'Say it to me in French.'

'*Mon seul désir*. Now you say it.'

'Oh, I can't!' said Rosa.

'Say it,' said Stephen, 'say it. I want to hear you,' and put out his hand, but no sooner had he touched her than Rosa seemed to grow smaller and shrink away from him.

'I'm sorry,' he said, stiff and hostile. 'I was only going to kiss you.'

'Oh, don't be angry,' pleaded Rosa, who did not know why she had done it. 'Please—' she cried in distress. 'I can't explain it but—'

'Why not?' he said without sympathy. 'Haven't you been kissed before?'

'N-no, only, when I was very young.'

Stephen stood thinking that William and the others had told him stories.

'You see,' said Rosa, in anguish that he might think she disliked him, 'when a man like you is – friends with a girl like me, it is usually for – that.'

'Is always for that,' William would have said.

'Besides, I have a feeling,' said Rosa, more truthfully than she had spoken in her life, 'I have a feeling that it might get serious for me. I think I couldn't help it and I should like you to break with me now while—'

'While?' He came nearer.

'While I can bear it,' said Rosa and presently, taking her courage again, she said: 'Those words on the sundial, "*mong serle daisir*"—'

'Yes,' said Stephen without smiling.

'You said they meant "My chief desire"?'

'Yes.'

'They are what I feel about you,' said Rosa simply and definitely, and stood waiting for him to speak.

'This sundial,' said Stephen at last, 'is about a hundred and fifty years old, a century and a half, Rosa, and all that time lovers all over the world have said to one another the same things you said to-night; after we're dead other lovers will go on saying them, and all that time they have made promises to each other. I believe those promises are here, now, where we shall promise too.

'I promise you, Rosa,' said Stephen solemnly, 'that I shall never be like – like the men you talk about. We shall be friends, I won't touch you unless you want me to, and if I do, if we decide to love each other, I promise you that I shall marry you before we do, or at any rate,' he added, 'immediately afterwards. Now will you kiss me?'

# 7

Rosa went to sleep that night with Stephen's words still in her head. 'Lovers all over the world have said ... after we're dead other lovers ... I promise you, Rosa,' and in her happiness she pitied them all, Belle who was so wrong, the sleeping auntie who had forgotten secrets and lovers and young and lovely men, and Blanche who was too young to know them. She lay thinking of Stephen and his promise and presently she fell asleep.

When she woke the room was cold and grey, there was another light outside the window, the garden was stirring, it was almost dawn. She had woken to something strange. She sat up. Belle's bed was empty.

Auntie moved, but did not wake. Blanche lay like a drugged fairy beside the giant that was auntie, wrapped in a cotton quilt, and there was Belle's bed blank and neat, the quilt turned down, her nightgown folded on her pillow.

Slowly Rosa's eyes went over the familiar room, the familiar things; a rubble of clothes on a chair, the glass of water with auntie's teeth in it under her bed, her table with her pin-tray and jewel-box, her *prie-dieu* set in front of the niche, the striped rug by the chest-of-drawers; and came back to the empty bed. She refused to look at it, but her eyes came back to it. She remembered how Belle had said, 'This is just the time I *am* going out with him.' With a pang and a sickening inward trembling, she remembered how Belle had looked when she had come in the night before, and she had deliberately chosen to do it again; he could insult her, hurt her, bruise her, tear her clothes off and because she wanted something from him she went back for more.

Rosa heard Belle saying, 'Get this into your head. It doesn't matter what we do because we have nothing to lose, we might gain ... Do anything to get you on, anything for money, anything to get you away from here ... We come from nowhere ... We are nothing.' Now Belle had put them down once and for all; she had dirtied them as well as herself.

That evening, that very evening, when she and Stephen had found the sundial, had been for happiness in Rosa's life like a holy picture that is bright at the edges; the finding of the sundial in their garden had given her faith in herself, had given her importance as if she were in history. She had said to Stephen, looking at the face of the old clock, 'How easy it must be to live if you know that you are someone.'

'We're all someone.'

'I mean someone worth while, someone great. To be born great.' Or even respectable, she might have added, or European, or rich, or any of those things her family was not. The sundial had brought her a crumb of importance, had lifted them up until Belle had done this, deliberately done it. She could not help it if it happened once, thought Rosa, but this, she chose this because she wanted something, money, clothes. I don't know, but I shall never speak to her again.

Quivering, she heard voices, someone talking loudly in the porch, and she threw herself down in the bed pretending to be asleep, for she did not want to see Belle, but no one came in. There was a sound of bumping and dragging as if something heavy were being carried out, and a sound of stamping and ring-ing steel that she could not understand.

Wide-awake she lay and listened, then slipped out of bed and stole through the sitting-room to the door, and cautiously opened it. She stepped out into the passage, and the porch was full of people.

At first she thought they were a band of Indian players, impu-dent to come so late into the house to do tricks and make money, until she saw that they were busy. Numbers of them, dressed in white with hats like halos of twisted cloth on their heads, were carrying boxes and trunks down the stairs and out on the drive, and some with tunics of crimson reaching to their knees over muslin pantaloons held torches that blew in the wind; the tossing light made fierce shadows on their faces and gave the crowd a wild inhuman look that frightened Rosa. She huddled herself against the passage wall.

There was one young Indian, finer than the rest, who was attended by two others with sashes of gold tied over their shoul-ders; he had a turban of apricot gauze, ruby studs in his ears, and he was giving orders to the others in a shrill treble, almost like a girl's, beating at them with a cane.

The servants went backwards and forwards like ants, they seemed tired and dumb like servants who have been kept up all night; Rosa could not think whose they might be, for she had never seen any like them. Pressing back against the wall she could see out into the porch, the torches shone on the back of a horse, its flank gleaming in a marbled pattern of bronze and black; she could see the legs of a man on the back seat of a carriage, its lamp reflected in the panels. Who could have opened the gate, she wondered? It had not been opened for years. From beyond, in the lulls between shouting and the din, she could hear the noise of the crows waking in the garden, and of a gharry passing in the street.

There was a dog, a small, white dog that ran in and out among the legs and feet, and stood on the steps barking at the horses.

The young Indian clapped his hands and suddenly there was quiet, the servants vanished, even the torches had gone and the porch was filled with only the cold dawn light, the marble floor was empty. Rosa heard footsteps coming down the stairs, light and slow, and voices speaking together. The steps sounded in the vestibule, and now it was one voice speaking, a girl's, and it seemed to Rosa that it was pleading, imploring, and then it changed to weeping. In answer came a man's voice, words that Rosa could not understand, and she thought that they were in a foreign language.

The girl spoke again, and again her voice rose and broke into sobs; the man said something softly and quickly, there was the sound of a kiss and his steps rang in the stones. He went so quickly through the porch that Rosa had not time to see him, only to catch the line of his cloak, the light on his hair, which was grey, and the phantom white of his legs that seemed to be in stockings.

A door banged, there was the crack of a whip, the sound of wheels grinding on the gravel and of horses' hooves, rising immediately to a trot. A girl ran into the empty porch; for a moment she stood poised above the steps as if she would fly after the carriage, then she seemed to crumple, took two steps and fell against a pillar, hiding her face with a strangled, choking cry.

Rosa felt a rush of blood in her ears, a pricking in her breasts, and along her thighs, a moment of icy terror. She was looking at herself.

As the girl had turned towards her to grope towards the pillar,

Rosa had seen her own face; it was *her* body that was sobbing against the stone, *her* hair had tumbled from its ribbon on to her shoulders, *her* voice had spoken. She wore her hair dressed in loops and curls, her skirts fell about her feet, a queer flowing dress, nearly violet in the grey light, the colour of the eyes in a peacock's tail or of morning-glory flowers, and with a stab of fright Rosa remembered that Robert had said that first: 'Blue, the colour of morning-glory'; as Robert had said, too, the dress was cut low, almost showing the breasts.

Her fright turned to a numbness in which she was not afraid; the cold breath that touched her and blew in the silk dress was only the wind, the light that filled the porch was only the dawn. She was not frightened now, though the blood was still beating in her ears and her hands were dry; then the little dog came running out, sniffed the girl's feet and lifted its leg against the pillar.

'Oh, Echo! Echo!' said the girl through her tears but it took no notice; it was like a pekingese on stilts, silky and white, and ran round visiting every pillar.

The girl raised her head. Someone was coming down the stairs, a man's footsteps, deliberate and strong, and on her face came such a look of terror and repugnance and horror that Rosa gasped. The girl looked round wildly this way and that, hovering, not knowing where to escape, and ran like an arrow straight to the passage where Rosa stood.

Rosa slammed the door, the passage floor seemed to swing up and she shut her eyes; she was in a tumult of fear and grief, she thought she fainted, for the girl seemed to run through the closed door and past her, she met with something live and fine as mist, and the girl's sorrow cut her own heart.

'*What* are you doing, slamming the door and waking the whole house?' cried Belle. 'Are you mad?'

'It's you, Belle, it's you,' stammered Rosa, putting out her hands to feel her. 'Oh, Belle! Belle!'

Belle shook her impatiently. 'You're walking in your sleep,' she said. 'Don't cling like that. Come back to bed.'

Rosa followed her back to the bedroom. All her anger had gone, only a sadness, a solitariness filled her. Her knees shook and she sat on her bed, leaning on the head rail, wondering how to tell what she had seen; she looked at Belle and the words were quelled on her lips.

Belle was white and haggard, even the colour seemed gone from her hair; she took off her clothes with little dragging movements, and she too sat on the edge of her bed, staring into the garden where the light was coming fast.

At first her body shone white, and as the light grew, it took on its colours, first a pearly then a rosewood tinge, with deeper points to her breasts and the shadows under them, and under her arms and between her thighs; between her breasts the skin was smooth and pale like the white blaze of an animal's chest. She shivered, her mouth trembled, but still she stared into the garden.

'Belle, do put on your nightgown.'

No answer.

Belle began to cry. She cried like a child, lifting her face, letting her tears stream down on to her thighs. Rosa came to her and timidly put her arm round her.

'Belle,' she whispered, 'dear Belle. Don't cry,' and it seemed that she had heard that sobbing before.

'I can't go on,' sobbed Belle. 'I can't go on with it, Rosa. I can't! I can't!'

'You're tired, that's all,' said Rosa. 'It will be better in the morning.'

What was she saying? 'You shan't go on with it,' she said loudly.

'Hush,' sniffed Belle. 'I haven't got a hanky.'

'I'll get you one,' said Rosa joyfully.

'No, never mind. I've used the sheet, but give me my night-gown.'

Rosa helped her on with it and pulled back the quilt. 'Go to sleep,' she said. 'Don't even *think* about him. You shall never see him again.'

'Go to bed, Rosa,' said Belle wearily.

'I'll stay with you if you like.' But Belle pushed her away.

'Belle, I—' said Rosa half in, half out of bed. 'Belle, you won't—'

'Oh, I don't know,' Belle answered hopelessly. 'What else is there for me to do? I'm too tired now to think. Go to sleep, please, Rosa,' and then she added defiantly: 'I shall though, all the same. I shan't spoil it now. I'm not afraid of him. Only he makes me hate—'

'What, Belle?'

'Nothing.'

Rosa did not answer, but lay looking at the light pouring into the room. Her mind felt strained and empty. The girl in blue and Belle, they were muddled in her mind. They both had that look on their faces; they wept, and then came that look of horror and repugnance. 'He makes me hate—' 'What?' 'Nothing.' What had she dreamt? Or did she dream? She knew that she did not. Why should she dream about a dog unless it were Blanche's talk?

'Belle, are you asleep?'

'*Now*, what is it?'

'To-night, I wasn't dreaming when you found me. I saw a ghost, Belle.'

'You always tell such lies, Rosa. Do go to sleep.'

# 8

Auntie had not been in ten minutes from the market before father began to speak about the girls.

They all loved going to the market, but it was very tiring, and as soon as she came in auntie had to sink into a chair and take off her shoes, wishing aloud that there were someone kind enough to rub her feet.

All their shopping was done in the market. Outside it, on the bricks, the pigeons picked up the grain that had fallen from the nosebags where the hackney-horses drooped in the shafts, their necklaces of blue and white beads falling over their ears. Behind the carriage-stand were the flower ranges, where almost every evening a wedding-car would be decorated, and where they sold bouquets and floral-baskets, wreaths and crosses, and ran after you with buttonholes to make you buy.

The market was divided into long ranges with Japanese-Woolworth-Americo-Birmingham shops in ranges; all the shops of one kind together, over all the hot tin roof and, under the jostling feet, endless stains of betel nut and spittle on the concrete floor.

To the right were the flower ranges, sports shops, trunks, Japanese curios, confectionery and food; to the left, books, tobacco, china, glass and goldfish, fruit and Chinese shoe-makers; at the back, toys and stuffs, hats, belts and fancy buttons and the meat market.

In the central aisle, beyond the silk and jewellery shops, the drapers called out 'Tape, 'lastic, button,' and in the centre were the brilliant cushion shops around the fire extinguisher and the weighing-machines. Everywhere the coolies, with their numbers on their shirts, carried parcels and boxes and tins in flat baskets on their heads, pushing through the crowd which pressed out to the entrance where they sold fur strips and feathers and cellu-loid toys. Round the cars came the beggars, old and blind, dumb and deformed, led by boys who whined and called out 'Mummie! Mummie!' They showed scales and leprosy and running eyes, tongues cut out at the root, and withered arms, and among them a sad old lady, dressed in a muslin dress and sandshoes and a toque, sold crocheted camphor-balls on strings.

There was nothing of any kind that had not its cheaper dupli-cate in the market, there was nothing there that could not be bought two pies cheaper in the next shop, and the bargaining for a piece of bread or six buttons could take an hour; but there was one superstition, the first customer of the day must buy to bring good luck, so that the early morning was the time to go shopping when bargaining was favourable and, in the produce market, the food was fresh.

That was when auntie went, every morning early, to buy the day's food, and as she picked her way from Hertford Lane across to the eastern aisles, she passed the bird-shops, where hundreds of canaries and love-birds and budgerigars were singing in their narrow cages, as if they were in Heaven, thought auntie, not set above this hot street of chattering, monkey natives. Now auntie could not think of Paradise and the angels without a flight of budgerigars with feathers of heavenly blue and white, the Virgin's colours, or canaries singing in a company, needing no harps to make their music.

It came naturally to her to think of Paradise in the market, for every morning before she came shopping, she went to Mass, and this was the only time of day she wore her hat.

Mass that morning had been long, and Father Ghezzi had detained her, for he too wanted to speak about the girls. Belle had not come to see him and they did not come to church. 'They used to come every day with you, Mrs Kempf, even little Blanche.'

'She is so weak,' pleaded auntie. 'Nothing I can do makes her robust. At first I thought it might be worms—'

Her voice died away under the Father's eye.

'All the more if she is weak and in danger,' he should have said, but looking at auntie's troubled face under the taffeta ears he relented, and said instead: 'I think, Mrs Kempf, that it would be good if you made a retreat.'

At that auntie flushed and trembled. 'It is the children,' she said, confused, 'and my brother-in-law, their father, he doesn't get on. I don't see how it is possible, Father.'

He sighed and left her; auntie felt she had been lacking in holiness and sighed as well, and in the market a piece of mutton she had marked for her own was snapped up by a fat mugh cook while she was actually bargaining for it.

And now father had started on the girls.

Father's scenes were noisy and dangerous, but they did not last; he could not hold an idea long in his mind. And now it was first the girls and the money he had wasted on a typewriter they were too lazy to use, and then, when auntie told them what the priest had said, it was why they had given up going to Mass.

'At least you should go on Sundays. Do you hear me, Belle?'

'I can't go on Sundays; how can I? I go out on Saturday nights.'

'You needn't drink after twelve o'clock.'

'And if I am late in?'

'I have known girls,' said auntie, 'who have taken their hats and coats and put them over their dance dresses and gone to Mass from the dance.'

'I should like you to do that,' said father.

'Why? You never go,' Blanche pointed out.

'I am not well in the mornings now. You know that, Blanche. All day long I toil and slave and no rest from pain, and then I must go to Mass as well. I would gladly go if I were able. It is my pain that prevents me.'

None of his family answered him; they had grown up with pain, only Blanche continued to stare at him dispassionately as if he were an insect and not her father.

Boy came in from the pantry, his duster over his shoulder, and put a tin of treacle on the table. Father dipped in a piece of bread he was eating and bit it off.

'You are simply disgusting,' said Belle in a choking voice, springing up from the table. 'You eat like a pig.'

'Sit down!' shouted father, but Belle walked past him to the door.

'You call me disgusting!' said father. 'You hear that, auntie? My own child calls me disgusting and pig in my own house. I who have kept her and cared for her and worked for her since she was born!'

'You never did any work in your life,' said Belle curtly. 'If we hadn't our mother's money we couldn't live.'

'That girl is an ungrateful little bitch!' declared father. 'You hear me, auntie? I shall have nothing to do with her any more. She may starve, but I shall pay nothing for her, nothing beyond what is absolutely necessary. I shall not speak to her again.'

Belle leaned in the doorway and smiled. 'You needn't worry. I've got a post.'

'You have?' cried Rosa. 'But you're not trained, Belle—' and broke off.

'You're very silly to take any piffling post. I have told you,' said father grandly, 'that I will find you a post. I have got great influence at Truscott, Wren and Co. There they *start* you with seventy rupees. What is this post?'

'Private secretary to Mr Harman. He has his own firm, something to do with the Standard Cable Co.'

'Private secretary!' said Rosa involuntarily, and stared at the tablecloth. Auntie looked from her to Belle, at Belle's pale cheeks and eyes that still showed that she had been crying.

'I think,' she said slowly and loudly, for she was not accustomed to speaking her thoughts aloud, 'I think that Belle is too young and she is not to be trusted. You should forbid it, Joseph, and I think that all of you ought to go to Mass, you too, Joseph. It is bad to forget your religion, and you girls, who will not listen, have only yourselves to blame. I found Belle's dress under the cupboard. She should not be a private secretary. You must forbid it, Joseph.'

'The pay is a hundred and fifty,' said Belle quickly.

'That is too much,' said auntie. 'They start at seventy.'

'You're not going to take it, Belle,' cried Rosa. 'You can't.'

'Why can't she?' Father brought his fist down on the table with a crash. 'All you women, chattering and talking and ordering among yourselves, I won't have it. You can talk, Rosa, when you can earn like your sister. Now she can pay back a little of what she has had all these years. A hundred and fifty will help us all.'

'A hundred and fifty is too much,' said auntie again. 'No young girl starts on more than seventy. She should not do it, Joseph. It is too much.'

'How can it be too much? You are so stupid, Anna, and did you bring a paper from the market for me? No, I thought not. I am not considered in any way at all. Now what am I to do all morning? Boy must go and get me one. Give me some money. Boy! Boy!'

Auntie felt old and sad as she drank her tea. She knew she should have watched Belle, but how could she, with tired feet and her mind that was old and full of so many things, keep pace with Belle, so determined and swift and strong? She had always been beyond auntie, who had brought her up, using her feebleness to protect Belle's strength, to protect all of them, and now she could do it no more. If Belle had been with a fast set she could have understood it, but Belle had been to parties with a girl from school. She was just out of school herself, and this had come, simply and swiftly, while auntie slept. A tear fell from her cheek into the teacup, and father said, 'My God! Must you cry? There is always crying in this house.'

Blanche immediately began to cry as well, for the sight of auntie's tears shocked her.

'You too!' cried father. 'Is there anyone who doesn't cry? Why are you not at school?'

'I'm not at school,' said Blanche scornfully, 'because my stomach is upset, and if I knew why it was I'm crying I shouldn't tell it to you.'

When father had gone to read his paper, she went down on her knees by the sideboard and took out a box from the bottom shelf; it was full of pictures of dogs cut out from *The Tail-Wagger*, *Our Dogs* and *Country Life*. Most of them she had stolen, turning the pages over and over on the market bookstalls and tearing out advertisements when the babu was not watching; she would slip her hand in and, looking the other way, tear out a strip in the right place. She was expert, but the blood beat in her ears and she could hardly walk away for her legs trembling, and at night the thought of being caught kept her awake. It was only her great love that drove her to do it.

'I wish I could find a picture like Echo,' she told Rosa. 'There isn't one like him anywhere.'

'Is he small and silky with butterfly ears?'

'He is, and he bounces,' said Blanche. 'He goes so high he might have wings; his eyes look like toffee-balls, and you know, he's naughty, he never does what he's told.'

'Did you see the lady?' asked Rosa carefully.

'What lady?'

"The lady with Echo.'

'There wasn't one,' said Blanche. She was not interested in ladies. Echo would not leave her when he was called, he planted his paws on her knee and looked at her with his laughing toffee-ball eyes.

77

**9**

As a secret Rosa showed Blanche the sundial. 'Who found it?' she asked, too awed to touch. 'Was it the gentleman?'

Rosa nodded. 'His name is Mr Bright.'

'That's a good name for him,' said Blanche seriously. 'He is bright, like an angel.'

'What a goose you are.'

'But he *is* like an angel,' Blanche insisted. 'Look at my holy card and see. He's just like Gabriel.'

'Perhaps he is,' said Rosa absently. 'Only think, Blanche, he says this has been here for more than a hundred years and that the house and the garden have too; all, all so old.'

'But the grass is new,' cried Blanche. Grass could not be as old as that, already she and the deSouzas had worn it bald, playing on it, and none of them could be called very old.

'I think, you know,' said Rosa, 'that this has something to do with Echo and the lady who called him. I think that Echo's a ghost.'

'How can he be? He's a dog,' said Blanche, and running indoors forgot it.

The sundial stayed hidden away under the jasmine, for Stephen and Rosa had put back the bricks and no one noticed the extra rubble. They wanted to keep it secret, but why neither of them could tell.

Stephen was still young enough to catch fire; he had not been buried by experience and he had always been singularly exposed. He had none of the common sense of his generation, and Rosa had taken him in two ways, by her strangeness and her pitifulness. She could have found no words to move him more than those, 'I should like you to break with me now, while – I can bear it.'

Rosa had beauty for him, too. He said she was like a ballerina, poised, with the small dark head that to him was essential in a dancer. 'I can't *bear* them blonde.' Sometimes he said she was like a rose, 'the small white kind you wear in buttonholes.'

He had beautiful comparisons for them all in those first days, even Blanche, in spite of her dark skin, for now that he came almost every day he had to see her. Rosa had been nervous about introducing her to him and she had known it. Stephen wondered why she was uneasy with him, defiant, and spoke to her in the way that made Janet worship him, as if she were as old and important as Rosa, as Mr Barton did.

'You remind me,' he said, 'of a little gazelle, so graceful with that delicate neck and those great eyes.'

Blanche did not know what he meant, but she was pleased, until Rosa said, 'Blanche says you remind her of an angel,' when she blushed deeply and walked away.

Now auntie knew him so well that she could forget in front of him and take off her shoes, and he had been very kind in lending her money for the bazaar, never asking her to pay it back.

He took Rosa out, to dance, to dinner, for picnics and walks by the river, and once on a queer expedition to the cemetery to look at inscriptions on the tombs. Rosa was used to cemeteries, she often went with auntie to visit her mother's grave, but this was the old burying ground in Park Street, and there was no one buried there that either of them knew.

With Stephen she walked through the silent aisles of that saddest of all cemeteries, where the dust of boys and girls lies under the heavy monuments and tablets, reading with him the young forgotten names.

'But they were all so *young*,' she cried. 'Why were they all so young? Hardly anyone more than twenty. Oh! they were so young to die.'

'I can't believe they died,' said Stephen. 'Even their names feel alive. Read them, and you begin to wonder what they were like, and by wondering you begin to know what they did, what they said, and then they seem to be going on now; alive, not dead, as if these graves were only the ending of a story that we know, there must be an ending, but the story does not die. Can you stand here, Rosa, and believe they are dead?'

'But this is a cemetery,' said Rosa, puzzled.

Stephen often puzzled her. For instance, he was always laughing at things that were not funny. Why did he laugh when he saw the 'Stop me and buy one' boys in their sailor suits with H.M.S. *Horatio* on their hat ribbons? And cyclists who had no lamps and carried a live wick in a paper bag; Rosa said it was dangerous, but Stephen said it was perfect.

Perfect! That was another thing. He said 'Isn't that perfect!' when they passed the Clean Head Wig Company, but he could not have meant it, because he laughed when he said it, and what was there to laugh at in a sensible name like that?

His sudden anger was as puzzling as his sudden laughter. He seemed to dislike most what Rosa liked and admired best of all, what she thought everybody must like and admire. He thought Lepri's, which to Rosa was paradise, rather dreadful; he did not like Shirley Temple, and he asked Rosa to take off her bangles, one dozen that her godfather had given her. He could not bear bangles, not even Blanche's, which she wore one on each sooty little wrist.

'But mine are gold,' said Rosa.

'That makes it, if anything, worse.'

He corrected her for saying things that were correct. 'Not a *smart* dress, Rosa, for God's sake.' 'Why do you say bee-hind, bee-fore?' 'Say tummy instead of stomach.'

He did not give her many presents, and when he did they were always rare and precious to him, with a meaning that usually had to be explained to Rosa; he never gave her safe ordinary things, and now she was afraid of not saying the right thing.

She remembered the clasp. It had been a buckle, he said, but it did not look like anything at all, and the stones were not real. 'They're paste,' he told her reverently, 'old French paste.'

'Paste,' echoed Rosa, and though she treasured everything that Stephen gave her, she was ashamed to show it to anyone. She took it to Hukimchand in the market and he polished it up nicely for her, so that it sparkled like diamanté and was really very pretty.

Stephen looked at her when he saw it as if she had done something obscene. 'Give it to me,' he said in a low, dangerous voice, 'give it back to me.' Rosa took it from the front of her dress and gave it to him without a word, and he threw it down on the floor and smashed it to pieces with his heel.

Rosa burst into tears, but she could not see what she had

done. 'How should I know it was valuable and historical?' she sobbed.

'*Stop* saying historical,' shouted Stephen, and more gently, 'It isn't a question of that, it's a question of taste. You can't see anything unless it's labelled.'

'You could teach me.'

'It's not a thing you can learn unless you have a feeling for it. You either feel it or you don't. I thought you might, you look so sensitive, but you don't. Stop crying, Rosa, you can't help being different.'

'If I were a foreigner you wouldn't mind if I were different.'

'You're not a foreigner,' he answered quickly. 'That's where I think you've all been so stupid. You won't be foreigners. You insist on being inferior Britons.'

'That isn't fair,' cried Rosa hotly. 'We are as much British subjects as you are.'

'That's what I mean. It's all so false. You're no more like a British girl than that poinsettia is like a daisy. You talk of going home to England, when the only home you have is here in India. It's such sham. Why can't you be content, more dignified?'

'Some of us are,' said Rosa. 'There are old good families like the Bartons and the Ramberts and some Armenians.'

'What about the deSouzas?' asked Stephen, smiling.

'I didn't mean the deSouzas,' said Rosa quickly. She resented that smile all the more because she would not defend Robert. She did not want Stephen to know anything of Robert; already he was too interested, and that was her fault.

In the first days, when he was still as much of a revelation and as little understood as a holy vision, she had asked him if he could help Robert to find work. 'He is clever, he only needs influence.'

Stephen was flattered, but Robert was furious when he heard of it.

'You might have spared me that,' he said, and his eyes were hard and cold as he looked at her; she had brought that hardness, that iciness into Robert's eyes, she was teaching him to hate, Robert who had been as pliant and sweet as a girl.

Stephen had said that. 'He's so beautiful that he's almost girlish; yet he isn't, he looks curiously strong. Very attractive, though, isn't he, in a Mexican guide fashion? Those lovely teeth. Why does he always keep away from me? He seems to hate me.'

'He's shy,' said Rosa treacherously.

'Do you know, I think he's queer,' said Stephen.

'He's not queer at all, he's very clever, but he can't find work and that makes him unhappy. He's unhappy, not queer, Stephen.'

'I meant sissy. I expect he has no use for women.'

'Perhaps not,' said Rosa weakly. She felt she was dealing the words like sharp little blows to Robert, and she hated Stephen for saying that hideous thing. Sometimes she did hate him when he ruthlessly cut her down, but he had only to smile, to say something absurd, to tease her gently, and she was his again. None of them could resist him.

Blanche said: 'I do envy you, Rosa.'

'Envy me what?'

'That Stephen.'

None of them saw him quite clearly, Rosa least of all. They saw his clothes, casual, sometimes shabby yet somehow elegant, his height and his brilliant hair; his hands, which were large with blond hairs on the backs of the fingers and beautifully cut nails. Rosa told them about his room, with photographs of his family and the dark, hazy house, but she did not tell them that there were photographs of girls, especially not of one called Catherine with gloves and a muff of violets. He had so many shoes and riding boots that he could not wear them out for years, all of them with trees of complicated yellow wood. Those shoes seemed to Rosa to mark the greatest gulf between them, and his cousin William's room was just the same.

'How many pairs of shoes has Mr Harman?' she asked Belle.

'Not many. Why?' answered Belle in the elaborately casual voice in which they talked of Mr Harman. Strange how, after the first shock, they had all settled down to the idea of him.

'Stephen has dozens and yet he's not nearly as rich.'

'He's probably poor,' said Belle, 'but he would have a great many shoes and shirts and handkerchiefs and underclothes even if he only had one coat. He's a different class, that's why.'

'What do you mean – a different class?'

'Caste, then.'

'You mean Stephen is a gentleman and—'

'Mr Harman is not. Yes.' Rosa felt immensely superior, but Belle said: 'That's one reason why I think you won't get very far with Stephen. The others are better for us. They are softer, kinder.'

'*Mr Harman* kinder than Stephen!'

'In the end, yes. You'll see!'

Besides his shoes the photographs made Rosa feel uncomfortable; his mother, his two sisters, Deirdre who was called D. and the smaller Janet, the one of the house with nannie in a corner of the frame and the ones of Catherine and those other girls. She should have been curious; she wondered enough, but instinctively she never asked questions about them, and avoided looking at them. When she went into the room she felt they were all alive, real, looking at her, and her eyes slid round to them though she tried to look away. She was always defending herself. 'I'm as good as you are, D. I'm *not* a bad girl,' and to his mother and nannie: 'You needn't worry. I shan't let him touch me – yet.'

Neither mother nor nannie nor Rosa herself were quite easy about that 'yet'.

It was true she had not let Stephen touch her, only occasionally kiss her, and then it was a light brushing kiss, such as he might have given his sisters D. or Janet. It was like the ban in a fairy tale, only Rosa knew no fairy tales; the one taboo they must not break, and from the beginning of the story it was plain that it would be broken, for otherwise there would be no story. Increasingly Rosa felt this, that as soon as she let Stephen love her it would be ended, the enchantment would be gone; it would never be the same again and his promise was like the happy-ever-after ending, not to be in a life like hers, that was too true to be good.

She did not know this clearly; it was a thing she felt, that made her deny herself to Stephen, and every day it was more difficult to hold out against him, for Rosa had hot blood. The least touch of his hand, his nearness when he bent across to shut the door of the car, the pressure of his body while they danced, the drive of his leg, firm and strong, against hers, set her blood racing. The more she felt, the more rigidly she penned herself and began to grow bad-tempered with him and try to quarrel.

With Stephen it was sweet and swift, and now at night he lay awake with a lingering lazy sleepiness that could not banish his excitement; it was like water lying placidly in the river, while underneath the currents kept it moving, pulling it down to the weir, running it faster and faster, until it crashed to the whirlpool below.

Stephen was in the whirlpool now and he was very uncomfortable to live with. Two or three times William began to speak, broke off and shrugged his shoulders.

Stephen must take it himself.

Through April into May the days grew hotter and longer, and longer and hotter. Now from dawn until sunset the hours were burning and slow and the electric fans whirled in the hot air, sending it down to dry cheeks and eyelids until they felt like paper. At night the sky changed from pale to powdered blue with hot wide stars, and still the fans turned and turned, fanning the hot air, until they were turning, ever turning in the brain.

Everywhere was a budding and blossoming, for this was the Indian spring. There were canna lilies in Benares colourings on the lawns, and the cathedral had skirts of garish unchristian colours; the creepers came into flower, scarlet and cream quisqualis, purple petria, bougainvillia in magenta and crimson, peacock purple morning-glory streaked with white and pink like native sweet-meats.

The jasmine buds opened into round sweet-smelling shapes, the oleanders had heads of fresh prim pink and there were crêpe flowers in Japanese mauves and magentas and frangipanis budded on their stiff ugly trees.

There was a glory of trees that came to perfection in May. Down Loudon Street and Rawdon Street, in every road and lane, the cassias, scarlet and orange and gold, were spread in a pattern of leaves like feathers against the sky, or more tranquil in pink and white, drooped their branches like weeping willows towards the ground.

Everywhere between the houses were the flowering trees, and

the houses kept their shutters closed to their foreign beauty. It seemed to Stephen that nothing in the city was quick except himself and the budding trees, that no one else saw beauty or knew love. He was in a fever and fidget of love, he could not be calm with Rosa because she would not let him touch her.

There was something beyond; the sensitive in him was searching for something beyond her; it was trying to fit a background for her, to make a décor for which the design was lost, lost or forgotten or overlooked. The words on the sundial haunted him, words he had read or seen or once heard spoken, 'MON SEUL DÉSIR'. 'Where have I heard them or read them? Where have I seen them? Oh! remember. Remember. Remember.'

Rosa had not told him that she had seen the lady in blue who was herself. She meant him to know, often it was on the tip of her tongue to tell him while he questioned her about the house and the sundial, comparing the inscription with the inscriptions in the Park Street burying ground, buying books on old Calcutta.

She kept it against him that she had not told him, and in some way it balanced her guilt towards Robert; she had not told Robert either, but he had seen it, too, and that made him in league with her, linked against Stephen, sharing something that Stephen ached to know.

She kept her secret as an insurance. Robert watched and waited, and Stephen wondered, searching endlessly, and never thought to listen to Blanche's chatter of a little dog called Echo.

Tigley Cross, Devonshire, and England had receded into a distant and colourless shore. In this heat, in this strange spring, there could be no England, and the letters that came from home were as meaningless as letters in an exercise book:

Very cold again, but the flowers have not suffered, the celandines in Dog Lane a sheet of gold. Daddy has gone up to town, it has turned so cold that I hope he won't get a chill, he has to be careful now. Nannie found your cricket boots, do you want them? If so I'll send them out.

And Janet:

Tom Bartlett was fined £2 for stealing five bantams. We made toffee because it was too wet to go out even for me. You'll be glad to hear that the schoolroom has new curtains, they are red and repp. I go back to Paris on Wednesday.

Celandines, red curtains. Daddy's chill. They belonged to a child Stephen, a child who had once lived in a house that brooded like a grey hen among toy trees.

There was another house now, high and shuttered above its broken walls. Now the palms hung still in the hot air of this strange spring, and the jasmine budded again over the words he could not find: *'Mon seul désir'*.

# 10

It was William who told him. In desperation one night Stephen asked Gray where they came from, '*mon seul désir*'! Gray might know, he read a great deal, but William said promptly, 'Tapestries. They're from those tapestries in the Musée de Cluny in Paris.'

'How do *you* know?' asked Stephen rudely.

'You don't deserve to be told when you speak like that, but I'll tell you. I think you've forgotten I was at school in Paris for a year. We used to be trotted round the museums and such like. They wanted me to be a diplomat until I convinced them that I was neither rich nor clever enough, and the words you are after, little man, are from a set of tapestries called *La Dame à la Licorne*.'

'I know! I know! I've seen them, only I've forgotten. William, you haven't a book or notes about them, have you? I can vaguely remember them, in rose and white, weren't they, with small flowers and animals scattered on them? Weren't they something to do with the five senses?'

'Yes, and the last one,' said William, 'is called "*à mon seul désir*", and no one knows what it means.'

'*La Dame à la Licorne*,' said Stephen thoughtfully. 'The Lady and the Unicorn. The Unicorn! Of course! Oh, William, of course, it must be, and they thought it was a leopard. The spear in its head is the horn. Still, I can't see what it means.'

'It's a symbol of virginity among other things,' said William, and winked at Gray. 'Is that the trouble?'

'Oh, shut up, William. Think. Was there anywhere on those tapestries, a shield with a cross-way band or what I should call it heraldically on it, and three crescent moons?'

'I don't remember a shield. Three crescent moons, did you say? My dear chap, there were at least two banners, or pennants, with crescent moons in each tapestry.'

'Good God!' shouted Stephen. 'It's *too* extraordinary. What connection could there *possibly* be between tapestries in the Musée de Cluny and a sundial in Bengal?'

'We might be able to tell you if you sit down and talk to us quietly,' suggested Gray mildly. 'All you do is to babble of unicorns and sundials and tapestries. We're giddy.'

'When I tell it,' said Stephen reluctantly, 'it sounds nothing. It isn't very much, but I have a tremendous feeling about it, a kind of compulsion—'

'Yes, I noticed that,' said William. 'I've had it myself, only I call it an urge.'

'How can I tell, if you're such a fool?'

'Stop it, William,' said Gray. 'Go on, Stephen.'

'I can only explain it,' said Stephen, 'by saying that it's like one of those dreams that get hold of you, that haunt you all night, and in the morning you can't explain what it was that you did dream. You know Rosa Lemarchant?'

William and Gray exchanged glances, but Stephen was looking at his hands, smiling as he thought of Rosa.

'She lives in an extraordinary house. Directly I went inside the gate I felt it. It's very old, high and narrow, with scrolled iron balconies like a house in a French town. It's grand, in spite of falling to pieces, as if someone of quality had lived there. The Lemarchants live in an annex, a small wing built out with an arched roof and windows, it might be a chapel, and over each window is a rough cast of a shield with a cross-way strip or whatever you call it and three crescent moons and an animal that might be anything, with what looks like a spear in its head. I see now it was the unicorn. Then in the garden under a pile of bricks and rubble, hidden by a creeper, jasmine, we found a sundial.'

'A sundial?' cried Gray. 'In India? Never!'

'It *is* a sundial. It's there all complete, only the hours are nearly obliterated, and on the pedestal, the shield and the unicorn are repeated, but the unicorn is practically defaced; and there are two initials, it's hard to tell what they are, but they might be a V and a B or an R. On the sundial, at the edge, are the words, "Duval. Bordeaux", which I took for the name of the maker, and a date, 1790, and on a minute tablet, hardly decipherable, there is an inscription, those words, "*Mon seul désir*".'

'Whew!' said Gray. 'No wonder you were interested. 1790, that was during the French Revolution. They must have been refugees. But why take a sundial away with them? Stephen, there's more in this than meets the eye. What are you going to do now?'

'I don't know. I'm waiting.'

'For what?'

'I don't know,' said Stephen again. 'Something will happen. That's the odd part. I keep feeling something has happened, is going on all the time, and I'm missing it. It's maddening.'

'Janet's at school in Paris, isn't she?' William put in. 'Why not ask her to go to the Museum and get a book or something?'

'Goody!' cried Stephen, 'I shall. She can send it out air-mail too.'

'Whom have you told?' asked Gray.

'No one.'

'Rosa will, though.'

'We promised each other we wouldn't.'

'Can't we see it?'

Stephen hesitated. 'Well, she doesn't know I've told you. I should have to ask her first. Perhaps she wouldn't mind. What do you think?'

'I think,' said William, 'be calm and don't get angry. I think you're getting mixed up where you don't belong, and you'd better stop.'

There was a silence and then Stephen said in an ominous voice: 'You mean Rosa, don't you?'

'Yes, if you must have it.'

'I can't help that.'

'Have you seen her people?'

'At first I thought they were terrible,' said Stephen earnestly, 'but when I came to know them better I began to understand. I wish I could make *you* understand. If you could get closer to them.'

'I'd hate to,' said William.

'That's it,' cried Stephen. 'You're all so bloody ladylike.' He appealed to Gray: 'Try and understand. They're fine people, Gray.'

'Fine?' asked Gray wonderingly. 'That's the first time I've heard them called that. Do you know what fine means, Stephen?'

'I do, and I still say it. Fine! Strong and' – he hesitated – 'sensitive is the nearest. Not all of them, of course. They've a pretty large percentage of waste. Not the father, he's bad, but the aunt and Rosa and some of their friends and Blanche the child.'

'Can a child be strong and sensitive?'

'Yes,' said Stephen firmly, 'she is. She's a contradictory, nervous infant and a dirty little beast, but she's fine; she lies, but she won't cheat, you can make her cry in a minute with a story, but she stands up to her drunken father like a stone. She's never had a chance, but she's fine, and so is Rosa, even that little bitch of Harman's, though she's losing it. She's hard.'

'She needs to be,' said William. 'I suppose it's no use telling you that you're asking for trouble?'

'None. I'm serious, William.'

William let that pass and said: 'Have they asked you for money?'

'No, they have not,' flashed Stephen, and turned crimson.

'That's a lie,' thought William, and said: 'You'll find it very expensive, but I'd pay for what I have if I were you. It's safer.'

'I'm not Douglas Harman!' cried Stephen.

'Douglas Harman would have the sense to do it. At least you would have that leg to stand on when you need it.'

'You're wide,' said Stephen; 'it isn't in the least like that.'

'I think you'll find in the end it's exactly like that,' William retorted, and Stephen went out of the room.

# 11

'Mother Celia spoke to me this morning,' said auntie, 'and asked why you, Blanche, had not been at school. I said to her that you had been, but you had not.'

'What's this?' cried father, and Blanche's face grew white and stony. 'You haven't been to school, eh? And why?'

Blanche muttered that she did not want to go.

'Want, want,' mocked father. 'Is want your master? Come here to me and I shall show you what you want. Lying and deceiving! You tell us where you have been or I shall beat you.'

'Don't frighten the child, Joseph.'

'I'm not frightened,' shouted Blanche.

'Well, tell us then what you did. Every day you left the house. Why didn't you go to school?'

'It's holidays.'

'Yes, to-day, but the holidays have only begun to-day, and Mother Celia says you haven't been for five days.'

'I shan't go to school,' answered Blanche in a loud voice, 'while they say such things about my sister. The girls say them all the time and Marie Fernandes said in the street that she is a –

94

a harlit and Mr Harman buys her clothes; and it is true so what can I answer? Sister Gerard said her name was not to cross our lips, and while they say that I *can't* go to school,' she panted, facing father like a little animal.

There was a silence. Father crumbled a piece of bread uneasily, Rosa was red and white by turns, but Belle looked at auntie across the tablecloth and smiled.

'See now,' said auntie in a whisper. 'See what you have done, Belle. What this has come to! Harlot! They called you that and it is true.'

No one answered her and presently she went on in that dragging whisper: 'It's you, Joseph, you are to blame for this. Hasn't Father Ghezzi told you to turn her out—'

'My own child, Anna,' he pleaded. 'She would starve.'

'Better to starve than to burn, and she wouldn't starve, you know that, Joseph; but that isn't what prevents you; it is because she gives you money, and whose money, Joseph? You should be ashamed. Is this something a child should hear? That her father will take money for his daughter. It's you who have brought us to this, your children shamed in the street, not daring to show themselves at school, and you,' she cried, turning to Belle, 'what do you care? What have you thought?' Belle continued to look at her, not answering, and auntie, with her face red and purple, screamed, 'Answer me or go. I will not stay in the house with you. You have ruined yourself, ruined yourself.'

'What nonsense you talk, auntie,' said Belle coolly. 'Am I ruined, I ask you? Am I?'

The old woman stopped short, glaring at Belle with angry eyes.

Belle's white tailored dress, navy striped handkerchief and

American sandals were as expensive as Belle herself; her hair was waved back at the crest of her head into curls, her nails glittered; on her little finger was a square aquamarine set in platinum, on the table lay her white antelope bag with her initials in brilliants.

Mr Harman's car fetched her each morning and took her to the office; she sent her change to his flat. Her account at the hair-dresser was paid by him, all the silk shops let her sign now they knew she was his friend, and the Chinaman, who before would not let them take their shoes away without the money, was not good enough now to make Belle's shoes, although he came to the house for orders. She had a cupboard with a long mirror and a set of enamel brushes and a huge bottle of bath eau-de-Cologne and especial pale pink towels.

Auntie had seen all this and thought that she must speak to father, but he was taking money from Belle and was pleased.

'Have you no shame, Joseph?'

'I'm very ashamed,' muttered father, 'but shame or not, it's done now. We can't undo it. You should have taken better care, Anna. Now you can watch out for Rosa.'

'Rosa!' cried auntie, flaring up. 'She, who brings her friend here so nicely and openly. Besides, Mr Bright is a gentleman.'

'Gentlemen are men, you know, Anna,' said father.

How could Rosa be blamed, with all that Belle had continually before her eyes? Auntie asked herself that. Stephen brought her a book, an old brooch, an ornament, but nothing more; auntie had to remind herself sharply of what she was thinking, for she found that she was saying that it was dull for Rosa. She whipped up her thoughts again, lashing Belle with her tongue, no thoughts were bad enough for Belle, no words. There was Miriam Rambert, so bold at school that they said she would never do good, there was Miriam engaged to a steady young fellow while Belle—

'Am I ruined?' said Belle in that insolent voice. Auntie gathered herself together for another attack.

'When Father Ghezzi came to speak to you, Belle, what did you do? You looked him in the face so brazenly and walked out without a word, you didn't even wish him. Oh, Belle, it breaks my heart. You could have married so well and settled down here so happily with your husband.'

'I'd rather die than stay in this place,' said Belle, and for the first time she spoke passionately. 'That is what you want to drag me down to, you and Father Ghezzi and all of you. You keep us here where we have no hope, the one place that is fatal for us. You can't help me and you won't let me help myself, but I shall in spite of you.

'What would happen to me if I were good, if I did "marry so well and settle down so nicely with my husband"? What happened to you, auntie? What happened to my mother? I would rather be you than her, at least you didn't bring into the world these babies, poor and wretched and unwanted like us. Look at Blanche. What can she ever do? How can she escape with that skin, that colour?'

'I don't want to escape,' challenged Blanche, quivering. 'I shall do with the colour I am,' and she ran into the pantry to hide her face with Boy, for she could bear no more.

'She can't escape,' cried Belle, 'but I can. I've been given only one thing, my fairness, my body, and I shall use it till I get what I want. I'll use it and none of you are going to stop me.'

Auntie was suddenly tired, almost too tired to care any more. She sat down and wiped her face. 'You don't know what you're doing, Belle.'

'Thank you. I know very well.' Belle had recovered herself. 'I know what I'm doing, auntie, and I'm doing very well.'

She picked her bag off the table, took out her case and threw a cigarette across the table to father: 'That's my last.' And father shamefacedly lit it and edged away to the veranda. She looked at auntie, who sat in her chair, her face turned away. 'Make auntie have some tea, Rosa,' she said, and passing to the door she put her hand on auntie's shoulder, but auntie jerked it off as if she had been stung.

Belle laughed. 'Rosa,' she called, 'if you'll iron my dress for to-night I'll give you those stockings I lent you.'

'I wouldn't take them,' said Rosa, but all the same she ironed the dress.

Two months ago she and Belle had gone to that party, only two months, and everything was changed. Belle and Mr Harman, Rosa and Stephen. Mr Harman and Belle had taken everything, she and Stephen nothing; a few kisses, light as leaves, and those she had brushed away, but as leaves are slowly driven into the earth, making it rich and ready, those kisses had gone deeper and deeper to Rosa's heart, warmed and mellowed her, and now she was ripe for Stephen. 'I don't want him to,' said Rosa to the iron. 'I don't mean him to, but if he were ever to start, oh! I'm afraid I should want him then.'

She laid Belle's dress on her bed and put the stockings defiantly beside it. Belle had plenty of stockings now; the first pair she had treated like jewels, and the belt that went with them she had bought in the market, pale green satin with green suspenders. Once she had let Rosa wear it.

'I shall never wear any of her things again,' vowed Rosa, but she knew that she would, for these elusive kindnesses were all she had left of Belle, and she could not refuse them.

## 12

All May the cassia trees dropped their glowing petals on the drive, spelling out the life of the flowers, petal by petal, letter by letter; they lay in heaps, disregarded, scattered into the drains, choking them up, and no one came to sweep them away. There was a sickly smell of decay, and the flies settled and swarmed over them, and the stench from the drains was worse than ever.

Mr deSouza was always out on his business when the tenants came to complain, and if he was written to, he cautiously replied that the letter had been received and its contents noted.

Robert had to write many letters in the fine pure hand which was among the useless things he could do to perfection, and often when his father was dictating, he would interrupt and tell him that the people were getting angry, the compound was filthy, the drains blocked and the flies disgraceful.

'Let them shift, let them shift,' said Mr deSouza airily, with a wave of his hand. 'I do not mind in the least.'

'You will mind with no money coming in for rent.'

'Something will happen,' said Mr deSouza, and now Robert thought of it, there was something in the air. His father had been very busy lately, coming and going, with strange people coming to the house and letters in long office envelopes brought round by peons. 'Something is going to happen,' repeated Mr deSouza, 'but don't tell them that. Tell them that certainly I shall attend to everything.'

'Unless you do there'll be trouble when the rains come. No water can get down those drains.'

The Mascareneses' baby was ill, from the heat or the smell of the flies. It had diarrhoea and cried all night; the sound of its crying penetrated to every corner of the house in those still hot nights; they could not hear it by day because of the band practising, but Blanche said it never stopped crying.

Mr Mascarenes seemed to grow even smaller, his sensitive little hands were always feeling for his handkerchief to wipe his eyes. When he was not practising he sat with Robert, for his wife kept him away. 'But she should let *me* do it,' he cried to Robert, his nice prune-coloured eyes swimming in tears, 'she is not gentle with the little baby. She picks him up roughly, shaking his stomach which must be very sore. She should pick him up "so",' he cupped his hands as if he were picking up a tiny china baby, and then wiped a tear away on his cuff because he had not time to find his handkerchief.

He had taken an engagement with his drummer, Juaneiro Dias, for piano and drums only; it was not at all the sort of engagement he should have considered, but they had to have money for the baby, Mrs Mascarenes said so.

It kept him out late at night; they were bound to go on playing while there were any people left in the club, and Mr Mascarenes often trembled with sick useless fury at the cruelty of these people who would not go home. While he smiled at them and played the tunes they asked for with his magical, clever fingers, he was hating them. 'God strike you dead. I want to go home to my little baby.' In the morning he was sorry he had thought such things, but he was so tired that he did not know if he had thought them waking or sleeping, or if the faces and the lights and the palms on the platform were real, or if he imagined the money that his wife took from him when he had hardly had it in his hand.

When he let himself in at the gate, the first sound he heard in the night was the baby crying, and his heart leaped, for he knew it was alive; as soon as he came in he took off his coat, infinitely precious as a part of his living, hung it carefully on a hanger, and took the baby from his wife. Up and down he would go with it until his shirt was wet with heat, and sometimes he sang to it until his wife told him to shut up; he had an idea that the baby liked him to sing; it put one fist in its mouth and listened instead of crying, but it would not let him put it down or sit down himself. Every night he was afraid his baby would die while he was not there, and thankfully he would go in from the cool of the garden, dew wet and colourless in the dawn, into the room that was hot and narrow and filled with the smell of a sick baby.

'Nita, shan't I not take him into the porch where it's cool?'

'Do you want to *kill* him? Do you want him to *die*? How selfish and thoughtless you are.'

Then one night, when he stepped through the door in the gate, he did not hear the crying; the garden was still, not even the palms moved, there was a hush upon everything. Mr Mascarenes stopped, the silence fell on his heart, his lips moved but he could not move. He stood, held by a cold, still fear. It seemed to him that, as he stepped through the gate, the porch had been full of people, figures in white that he took to be angels, and as he looked they were gone; and he stepped to one side as a rush of wind went past him, with a jingle and thud of horses' hooves and the sound of wheels on gravel and, though he could never be sure, he thought they drove straight through the gate.

He had seen angels, and though this sounded a very large carriage for a baby's soul he was filled with anguish and wrung his hands.

In his tiredness and his tears he went on up the drive, stumbling a little, and there was Rosa waiting, come to break the news to him and crying herself with her face hidden against a pillar.

'I know, Rosa, I know,' he was saying, but as if she could not bear him a look of horror came into her face and she slipped past him and ran into the passage; he heard steps on the stairs, but no one came, only a dog he had not seen before barked at him, scampering round before it too rushed away.

He went into his room and the baby was better and sleeping. 'Why was Rosa crying, then?' asked Mr Mascarenes in wonder, still pale, his voice quivering in an odd way; his wife, who was angry at being wakened from the first sleep she had known for nights, shrugged and lay down. 'How should I know? It couldn't be Rosa, for she is sick with fever and a bad stomach.'

'Fever!' cried Mr Mascarenes. 'She was in a ball dress.'

He told Robert, and Robert went thoughtfully away, for he remembered a dress that he knew was blue, and he was thinking that Rosa had no little dog that scampered and barked and rushed away.

Blanche had often talked to him of that dog. She wanted a dog so fiercely that she could no longer bear to go on the maidan and pet other people's dogs; now she had nothing of her own, not even Edward.

'And there is this little dog,' she told Robert. 'He seems to belong to no one, for I've never seen anyone with him.'

'He belongs to a lady in a blue dress,' said Robert. 'She is very sad, for each time I have seen her she was crying.'

'I wouldn't cry if I had a little dog,' said Blanche stoutly. 'But where does she live, for she doesn't live here, Bob? I have been up the back staircase and asked the sweeper at everyone's place and no one here has a dog like Echo.'

'If auntie catches you on the back staircase she'll beat you,' he teased her. 'I'll tell her.'

Blanche only grinned, for she knew he would not, and when he called her back and asked her, as if he pretended he did not want to know, how Rosa was, she told him kindly that she was still sick. 'Her stomach pains her,' she said and watching him, she added: 'Stephen is going to fetch the doctor for her.'

But it was for Blanche herself that the doctor was fetched. In a few days Rosa was better, like the Mascareneses' baby, but in June, in the breathless oppressive days before the rains broke, when the air was stale and heavy with dust and the wind was hotter than the still air, and the colour was scorched from the grass, and the paint blistered on the shutters, there was an outbreak of sickness among the tenants on the ground floor.

The very beauty of the flowering trees had brought the sickness, the petals rotted in the drains and the flies were black upon them, feeding on them, swarming into the house. The house seemed to sink in upon itself, the weeds that should have choked in the heat fed on the decay and thrust up through the stones cracking the plaster; on one of the pillars the cracks had made a face with a sickly smile; a shutter came loose on its hinges and clapped backwards and forwards, and nobody came to mend it.

Old Mr Barton had dysentery. Mrs Barton and Désirée sat silently in their sitting-room waiting for the nurse to come out, then they would rise to their feet like schoolgirls in front of a teacher and whisper: 'How is he?' He would not let his wife nurse him. 'Let me be quiet, let me be alone,' he said, and sent her away. It was the first discourteous thing he had ever done. Mrs Mascarenes had dysentery too, and had been taken to the hospital. Now their suite seemed quiet, for the practising and the baby's crying were gentle noises after the scolding voice of Mrs Mascarenes.

Then one night Blanche called: 'Auntie, wake up. Oh, please wake up, auntie. I'm sick. O auntie, my stomach.'

She called in a shrill thin voice as if the words were sharp and hurt her; she woke Rosa as well as auntie, and when they touched her she was fever-hot and dry, even the bed-clothes where she had lain were burning.

'It's the same as they all have,' cried Rosa. 'It begins this way. Where is the thermometer?'

Auntie had no thermometer, she had not had one for years, and she argued with Rosa, who said she must get one. How could she get a thermometer in the middle of the night?

'It's nearly morning,' argued Rosa; 'you must wake father.'

'Wake *father*. Are you out of your mind, Rosa? He is so tired at night. How can you?'

Blanche wanted iced water, and Rosa went into the pantry to find some, but there was not even a small piece of ice among the bran in the sacking where they kept it. The water was tepid when she brought it in the glass, but now Blanche did not want it. She was doubled up with pain, drawing her legs up convulsively, screwing herself around in the bed, and auntie stood by her saying, 'Try and sleep like a good child. Perhaps in the morning you'll be better.'

Suddenly Blanche burst into sobs. 'Oh, my stomach, my stomach. O-Oh-Oh, auntee!' And from her bed came a loud explosion and an indescribable smell. She clutched at herself, and auntie flung back the bed-clothes.

'Blanche! You filthee, disgusting child!'

It was then that Belle came in and found them; auntie outraged, scolding in her nightgown that was split up the back, Rosa pleading, 'She's ill, auntie, she's ill,' and Blanche exhausted on the bed, her face green-white, her eyelids fluttering, the clothes on the floor, the glass of water upset, the foul smell.

'What is this?' asked Belle from the doorway in her cool clear voice, holding her chiffon skirts away from the dirty room. Over her shoulder she called: 'Don't go, Douglas, I want you. Wait there.'

'How she orders him about,' thought Rosa, marvelling, 'and his name's Douglas. I never thought of him having a name.' Aloud she said: 'She's ill, Belle. She's very ill. Auntie scolds her, but she can't help it. My God! she's doing it again. What are we to do?'

'You must get a doctor,' said Belle, making no step to come into the room. 'Douglas will get one. Take those clothes off her bed, auntie, and put them outside. Rosa, get some newspapers and a towel and put them under her.' She stood there telling them what to do; she sent Mr Harman to fetch a doctor, she told auntie to dress and do up her hair; she told Rosa not to be hysterical; and they worked, choking back their terror, for now it seemed that Blanche would die of exhaustion before the doctor came. Their hands trembled with fright and still Belle stood there urging them on; she held a handkerchief up to her nose, her bracelets glittered in the electric light that showed every line of her lovely, painted little face.

'Go and wash your face,' she said to Rosa. 'The doctor will be here in a minute and you don't want to look a sight. This is the office number, if you want anything you can phone me.'

'You're not *going*?'

'I'm not staying here with this going on, thank you. I only came in to fetch a clean dress. Give it to me, please. I don't want to dirty myself. The doctor will tell you what to do, and I'll send you some money.'

'But – but she might die, Belle,' said Rosa, taking the dress off its hanger with shaking hands.

Belle's glance at Blanche seemed to say that she could not help that.

'You can't go, Belle,' cried Rosa, following her to the door. 'You can't leave her like this.'

'I told you I only came in for a minute,' said Belle testily. 'I'm not going to stay here with a sick child in my room. I've done all there is to be done, you and auntie are here.'

'But don't you care? Don't you care if she dies? Doesn't that matter to you, Belle?'

'The doctor's coming. Let me go, Rosa. You're crushing my dress.'

'I'm glad. I shall crush it. Thinking of a dress when your sister's dying. A dress!' said Rosa between her teeth, and she snatched it from Belle and threw it on the floor.

'You little fool,' said Belle, 'do you think that can stop me?' and she smacked Rosa's face with all her force, knocking her against the wall, and walked out.

Rosa's hands flew to her cheeks where Belle's hand had left a burning mark. 'You're a beast!' she shouted after her. 'A heart-less little beast.'

Belle turned and snapped: 'At any rate I'm not a helpless fool; you did nothing till I told you,' and Rosa was glad of those angry words, glad even of their quarrel, of anything of the quick warm Belle she used to know.

As Belle left the room with that 'Beast, beast,' ringing in her ears, and stepped into the passage, she thought that someone ran past her. Someone warm and fragrant as herself, with a rustle as of silk and a sobbing that might have been Rosa behind her, and an unfamiliar feeling seized her, a passion of fear and grief that she had not known before; for Blanche, for herself, for Rosa, she could not tell. She stopped short, torn by it, wondering if she should go back; but as quickly as it came it left her, left her sad and shaken, and she went out to the car. Mr Harman, who had not seen his little cat cry before, was startled.

'Is she very ill?' he asked in an awed voice. 'Is it infectious? Don't you think we ought to wait and see the doctor?'

'No, no. Go quickly,' cried Belle. 'Hurry. Take me away from here.'

Auntie did not like that doctor, he came asking questions and poking into her private affairs, making her feel very embarrassed.

'Do you boil your water, Mrs Kemp?'

'Kempf,' corrected auntie with dignity, 'my husband was a German from—'

'Do you boil your water?'

'Yes. Oh, yes, doctor, always.'

'Do you see it boiled?'

'Ye-s, doctor.'

'Every morning?'

'Well, perhaps not every morning, doctor, for you see I have to go to Mass and then to the market—'

'Let me see your kitchen.'

'At present we are using the pantry,' said auntie, agitated, 'and at present, with Blanche being sick, it isn't quite as tidy—' But he was in the pantry already, shouting out, 'Where do you keep your meat? Why haven't you a safe?'

'Well,' said auntie, trying to smile at the doctor, 'well my

brother is going to buy me one; at present I keep it on a plate, a
*clean* plate,' she added hastily, 'with a nice piece of muslin—'

'Filthy!' shouted the doctor. 'You people never learn. No
wonder that child is ill.'

'She's always been most healthy; it's just when she has these
stomach upsets—'

'She's got dysentery,' said the doctor in a dry, cutting voice
that chilled auntie to the heart, 'acute amoebic dysentery, and
what do you expect, Mrs Kempf? Look at the flies. I tell you,
look at the flies, and these drains stink.'

'The drains,' said auntie, and the words came oddly, now
high, now low. 'The drains are *not* my fault.'

'Have you had the health officer?' asked the doctor coldly.
'Who is your landlord?' and he went on asking questions and
putting down the answers in his little book.

'Is it dangerous?' asked auntie, and her voice was almost gone.

'Very,' said the doctor, snapping his book together without
one word of comfort. Auntie went back into the pantry so that
he should not see her face.

'Let her get better, Blessed Mary, Blessed Mother of Mercy.
The drains are not my fault. Make her better and I will put it in
the paper. I promise I will put it in the paper.'

From the Corporation men came to spray the drains and the
whole house smelled of chloride of lime; they climbed upon the
roof and examined the water tanks; they opened the drains and
cleared the rubbish. Mr deSouza had letters and visits from the
health officer; he did not care at all, but seemed busier than ever
on his own affairs.

'You must care, with all these people ill,' said Robert. 'It's a
scandal. They'll make you do the repairs.'

'Repairs!' scoffed Mr deSouza, rubbing his hands. 'With what I have told them they will be perfectly satisfied, and they are sure to delay a little and then I shall delay a little, and then you see—'

'Meanwhile these people will die.'

'They may not,' said Mr deSouza. 'I hope they will not,' he added earnestly, 'but if I have no money can I help it if they do?'

'You've got plenty of money,' said Robert slowly. 'It will be our fault if they die. I shall have to tell the officer you have plenty of money and all you do is to hide it up while people die.'

'And what do you do?' asked Mr deSouza. 'Nothing, nothing at all. If I had not to keep you I might have money for repairs; you keep a quiet tongue in your mouth, if you don't want me to put you out.' He smacked Robert on the side of the head so hard that he hurt his hand, and Robert let him do it without a murmur, as he had done all his life.

Robert was unhappy. He was haggard from want of sleep, for he helped at night with the Mascareneses' baby, and all day and all night he tormented himself with thoughts of Rosa and Stephen, Stephen and Rosa. Through the long hours when the hot blue night pressed against the windows he imagined her in Stephen's arms, her lips, that she had hardly let him kiss, given to Stephen, her body, that he had been afraid to touch, taken by Stephen. The scent of the jasmine, unbearably sweet, followed him as he walked up and down the Mascareneses' suite holding the baby, and always in his tired brain, with his thoughts of Rosa, the remembrance of that other girl troubled him. There was something he had seen or had not seen, Mr Mascarenes too. What was it? Robert could not remember. Echo was in it, but who was Echo? Was it a dream, or the echo of a dream, or was it Blanche talking? An echo of a dream told a long time since, an echo of words that somewhere someone had spoken.

# 13

Mrs Anthony, the Madrassi ayah, came to help to nurse Blanche, and in the evenings she stayed late gossiping with auntie, for Mrs Anthony loved a good gossip even more than the tea and chew of betel she would presently buy from the pan-seller on her way home. She wanted to find out from auntie where Belle had gone.

'She has gone for a secretary to a gentleman,' said auntie guilelessly, and Mrs Anthony's eyes narrowed. And who was Rosa's friend, this tall English boy? Mrs Anthony wanted to know that.

'He very pretty,' she said to Rosa, 'his hair like moonshine.'

'You mean sunshine.'

'Too pale for sun, but he very pretty sahib.'

'Am I pretty?' Rosa teased her.

'Very pretty, darling. So pretty, my Missy Rosa!' said Mrs Anthony, who did not think so at all, too thin, too dark and little; she liked a blonde, fat cheeks, dimples and curves, in a blue dress with sequins and pink roses.

Rosa was very pale, the last of her colour had gone in the heat and the strain of Blanche's illness; her eyelids had a lilac tinge that gave her a look of fragility, and she seemed to Stephen like a flower at night when the dusk has taken its colour and hidden its leaves in darkness, when only the shape of the flower is left, a ghost of itself.

There was something of dusk in these days. The rains were late, but for a week the sky had shown no colour, only a brooding grey, and the sun had not come from behind the clouds. The city seemed like a dream under that heavy sky. Stephen in his office, Rosa going about the house, were part of that dream, caught in each other; when Stephen came in the evening he could not bear to meet her before other people and he called her into the garden.

In the garden those Indian nights, it was hot and still and the moon was full, the parting of the palms shone like silver in the brilliantined leaves and the cassia trees dropped their petals on the drive with a sound like footsteps pattering up it. Everything had its shadow on the grass; the flying foxes across the sky, the convolvulus along the palm stem, the shadows of lily spikes and cockscombs and the steps with angles of darkness; and the shadows of Rosa and Stephen walking on the grass beside the sundial, where the jasmine was in full flower on the stone.

A firefly rested in the dark leaves, circled to the trees, and Rosa, watching it, said: 'Look, Stephen, a flying star,' as seriously as in a dream. If a star had blown down at her feet, she would have picked it up and given it to Stephen without surprise.

They walked now without talking, not looking at one another, not touching their hands. Stephen felt a spring of love and tenderness for this small Rosa, the anguish had gone, he had come to quiet and surety. In her a tide crept up, strong and fierce, and now it did not frighten her but filled her with a strange deep joy.

Then walking together, they seemed to change, for Stephen began to tremble, and Rosa to withdraw, he was eager, she reluctant, as if the garden held her, told her that love can be unkind as well as kind, that this was her time for dreaming, that she was not ready yet. She turned to Stephen as if she would say: 'Don't hurry me, Stephen. Let me stay, let me hold this dream of love for a little longer only in my arms,' and for the first time he swept her into his and kissed her on the mouth.

Auntie sat by Blanche's bed while Mrs Anthony rubbed her feet. Blanche lay, never still, tossing and muttering and crying out for a little dog she wanted. She had kept them going to and fro all day in this heat, and auntie's feet were again like boils. Mrs Anthony caressed and squeezed them in her black hands, drawing the toes out one by one so that they cracked, giving auntie shudders of pleasure.

A firefly came through the window netting, Rosa's star blown from the sky, and, as at a signal, the old women peered into the garden, but Stephen's hands were in his pockets and they sighed and returned to one another. When Rosa came in they were talking of curry.

'The doctor he asks me,' auntie told Mrs Anthony, '"What do you give them to eat, Mrs Kempf?" and I told him I always buy fresh in the market, and for breakfast I myself make a curry. "What, every day?" he said, and you know, Mrs Anthony, that master must have his curry, and how can I get different for the others with the little I have for the bazaar?'

Talking of curry on this night of scent and fireflies and moonshadows! Rosa, with Stephen's kiss on her lips, could not bear them or the room, the heat, the creak of auntie's chair, the smell of disinfectant and Mrs Anthony's musk. Though she had said

good night to him, she ran after Stephen and found him in the
porch where the pillars were milky in the moonlight. As she ran
he stepped out and caught her, and it was not the pale flower
Rosa he held, but a little eager animal; her hair brushed his
cheek, springing against his eyes, and she kissed him with small
sharp kisses like bites.

'Come home with me, Rosa,' he said, speaking soft rapid
words into her ear. 'Come back with me. I can't bear it any
more. Come back with me, Rosa.'

Rosa drew back and looked into his face.

'William?' she asked.

'He's away. He's down at the mill. Don't be afraid. I won't
hurt you. Please come, Rosa. Please. It will be quite all right.
Please come.'

Rosa put her fingers on his mouth and kissed them. 'Come
then,' she said, 'and don't talk any more.'

'You let her go?' asked Mrs Anthony. 'I think better you call
her back, madam.'

But auntie was too comfortable to care; her body felt heavy
and comfortable like a mattress, a mattress to sleep on, it was an
effort even to listen to Mrs Anthony. 'Rosa is a good girl,' she
said; 'she is a good girl and her friend is nice.'

'All good girls till they want to be bad,' said Mrs Anthony. 'I
think better Miss Rosa she come to see old ayah first.'

Through auntie's tiredness the words seeped down like poison
into her mind, and she kicked Mrs Anthony with the foot she
was holding. 'Disgusting talk!' she cried. 'I could take you to the
priest for that.'

'Priest!' hissed Mrs Anthony, puffing up like a cobra and
drawing her sari over her head for a hood. 'What you do,
madam, with Missy Rosa if her menses not come this month?

What you say to the priest when the child is born? What you do then? You want Mrs Anthony then, madam, and she not come, not where she kicked and scolded for telling truth. Give me my money, I go. I not coming back.'

When Mrs Anthony had gone, and auntie had to give her the last of Belle's money and the money she had saved for her thank-offering, when she had gone it was very quiet. Auntie looked at the familiar walls; the plaster was cracking over Blanche's bed, she must be moved or when the rain came the wall might come down on the poor child. She must be moved to-morrow, not now, not – now—

The lamp that burned in the niche by auntie's table on which she kept her pin-tray and her jewel-box with her ivory beads, sent a ray of light, and to her closing eyes she swam in light and there was a smell of musk, like incense. It seemed to her that the sky, moon-blue outside the windows, was the blue of Mary's robe, adorned with gold of stars or was it of fireflies? The rays that came from her sacred hands and about her head were stretched in beatitude to auntie worn out with watching and anxiety, auntie who had given Mary's money to Mrs Anthony. 'But I promise it all the same,' said auntie. 'Our Mother of Mercy, I shall put it – in – the – papers.'

She half awoke when Rosa, or was it Belle, came in; startled out of sleep when she saw her run and fall on her knees by the table under the niche; she was crying, and her hands clung to the cloth and her forehead leant against the table. It was Rosa, for her hair was dark, why had auntie thought that she was Belle? Why was Rosa wearing a dress that auntie had not seen before, with her hair in curls like some fancy dress? Then auntie saw with a thrill of her heart, that from her table her things had vanished, her pin-tray, her jewel-box, and there was a spread of lace and brocade fringed with gold, a crucifix, candles burning and lilies in tall vases.

Stiffly auntie let herself down from her chair on to her knees and bowed her head. She shut her eyes, and presently, when she opened them again, the vision was gone, her pin-tray and jewel-box were back again on the table, the lace and the gold and the candle flames had vanished. On her knees auntie wondered what the vision could have been, what holy saint had visited her; she thought it could not be the Blessed Mary, for she would hardly wear her hair in curls, besides auntie had always seen her in a headcloth, and the dress, though blue, was surely too bright and cut too low for Our Lady.

She thought then that it might have been sent as an earnest of repentance for Belle, or a warning, and as that thought came into her mind, with a shock she remembered Mrs Anthony's words, and that Rosa had gone out with Stephen.

She helped herself up from her knees, clinging to her chair, for she could pray no more; what use to pray when it was done. She sat down in her chair, a blankness of despair in her mind. 'There is bad blood in us,' she whispered, 'bad blood. Belle, now Rosa – and I thought Mr Bright was so kind.'

She could not exactly blame Rosa, she was a little in love with Stephen herself, for his hair and his laughter and his spoilt ways, but it was more terrible to auntie that Rosa had done this than that Belle had gone after Mr Harman. Belle had never been a good girl; she could look after herself or see that Mr Harman did, and he was rich, but Stephen was poor and could not do much for Rosa. 'It will all come on the family,' groaned auntie, rocking herself backwards and forwards, 'and I didn't think Rosa, my Rosa, would do a thing like that,' though she supposed, when you came to it, it was the same if you were married or not.

Why her girls, auntie wondered? There were plenty of nice respectable girls in Calcutta; look at Miriam Rambert, that thorn in auntie's flesh. Robert had been in love with Rosa, and though they were children and the families were not speaking, he would have married her. Now suppose anything happened, what would they do? Even Mrs Anthony had gone. People would say, 'They have bad blood, those Lemarchant girls.'

When Rosa came in she ran the gauntlet. There was Robert watching from his veranda, and auntie sitting up for her.

'Auntee! not in bed yet? It's nearly morning.'

She had no shame; she knelt where Auntie herself had knelt to pray, and lifted the old woman's hands and laid them against her face, and it seemed to auntie that she held a star in her hands, or a flower. It was shameful, shameful, but she could only look offended and say: 'Mrs Anthony won't come back. Better pray.'

'You're asleep,' said Rosa, and put her hand on auntie's lips; she would have kissed it but she remembered that was how she had kissed Stephen long ago, was it years ago? – now she would kiss no one else, ever again.

Her body quivered and hurt. She was bruised and crushed by love.

'Do I hurt you, my little love. I meant to be so gentle, but you're so lovely.' And she had cried: 'Hurt me! Hurt me, Stephen,' and afterwards courteously she had said: 'I'm afraid I wasn't very much good to you, Stephen.' He had laughed as he sat up on the bed and said: 'Ah, it's something you have to learn, is love.'

'I'm not asleep,' said auntie. 'I had a vision, Rosa. It was a miracle, that is why I said you had better pray. I tell you for your own good. A saint, a woman in blue—'

'That is not a saint,' cried Rosa, sitting back on her heels and staring at auntie. 'She was a ghost. I've seen her too. I'll tell you another time, but not to-night. Don't ask me to-night. Oh, I'm so happy, auntie! You can't believe how happy.'

'I don't think you ought to say so even if you are,' said auntie, deeply shocked.

# 14

In the morning they heard that Mrs Mascarenes was dead.

'Dead! Do they *die* of it, auntie?' Rosa cried in panic.

They looked at one another across Blanche's bed and at her with new eyes; for the first time they saw how emaciated she was, only a covering of skin over her bones, and that skin had curiously lightened to a grey earthen colour as if already she were dust, and there was a purple discolouration round her eyes and nostrils.

'Why didn't you let her go to hospital?' cried Rosa violently.

'In hospital you always die,' said auntie. 'I have never known anyone who went into hospital and didn't die. You see now Mrs Mascarenes is dead.

'The weather is so oppressive.' She went to the window. 'If the monsoon would break Blanche would be better. I think it will rain before the funeral and that will make it very difficult for them. It's difficult to pack the earth tightly enough if it's raining.'

'Stop! Stop, auntie!' Rosa wailed. 'Don't talk about it. How can you when Blanche is dying? Oh! why didn't I think of it earlier? I was thinking of – ' she stopped sharply, ' – while all the time – and now it's too late,' and at that auntie remembered she was not speaking to Rosa and went out of the room.

Rosa was not feeling well; she lay down on the bed opposite Blanche, and even now, when death had come close, she thought of Stephen.

She could not help it, she tried to fix her thought on Blanche, but the thought of Stephen came between. At first that thought was blissful, warm and tender, glowing in her heart, and then, as the days passed and he did not come, it sharpened with anxiety and fear. 'Why didn't Stephen come? What was wrong? Why didn't he come?'

In the slow days of that week Blanche lay alone making her solitary, unimportant fight, for auntie had not taken it in and Rosa thought only of Stephen.

The doctor came, sometimes twice a day, and auntie wondered how his visits would be paid for or the expensive medicine and arrowroot he ordered. He stood looking down at the straight little shape that was Blanche under the sheet, and shook his head, and in his look was a pity that changed to anger and impatience when he looked at auntie.

Mrs Mascarenes was buried and Mr deSouza sent a wreath of lilies that had turned brown in the heat like poisonous flowers. Now that the first zeal of the Corporation had been spent, a smell like decayed lilies hung about the house unless the doctor came, when Boy put chloride of lime in the drains and then went out with a cigarette tin and gathered it up again, for 'chloride of lime is very expensive,' said auntie, 'and I'm sure it's all nonsense.'

There were wind storms that filled the house with dust and rubbish, and teasing voices shouting above the wind which sank suddenly into a dull, hot stillness; there was a yellow light in the sky so that the grass changed to sage colour, and the marble of the Victoria Memorial was stained with yellow, and the tarmac on the roads was dark and dull as iron. The wind storms swept up with blisters of rain which ceased abruptly, leaving litter in the streets, raising the dust; night and day were heavy and hot, everything was slowed down, waiting for the rain.

Every day they said the rains would break, and night came and still no rain. A lethargy fell on the city under those leaden skies from which there was no escape. Mr Mascarenes had taken the baby to its grandmother, Mrs deSouza lay on the sofa, sending the children to fetch more ice, and the children were too oppressed to play; Mr Kawashima sat out in only his shorts, his yellow chest glistening with sweat, the Bartons' suite was shut for they had gone to Darjeeling. The Bengali family on the first floor shuttered their rooms and played endless Bengali records, the nasal music filtered into every corner of the house now that the Mascarenes band was no longer there to drown it. If it had not been for the doctor, auntie would not have done her hair or changed her slippers, but she never knew when he was coming, for he continued to attach this strange importance to Blanche.

Each time she heard his footsteps Rosa started up and then sank back in her chair, for it was only the doctor; she would bite her lip and stare at the carpet, not to cry in front of him, and in seven days her face had grown sharp and her eyes hollow with watching.

'To look at you,' said father, 'you would think we had death in the house.'

'Perhaps we have,' said Rosa, starting up, 'and what do you care if Blanche dies?'

'Why should she die?' Father almost said: 'She never died before,' but altered it hastily to, 'One person dies and at once you think that everyone must die, too. You will please not be so silly, Rosa. Go and wash your face and attend to your typing.'

Rosa, thankful to have escaped with that, fetched the type-writer and sat at it, staring at the keys.

If only she could write a letter to Stephen and ask him why he had not come; if only she knew, she thought that she might bear it. For seven days he had left her alone, and what had she done?

Over and over again she searched her memory of that night to discover what she had done. She had been willing enough, perhaps too willing, was that it? The painful colour came into her cheeks. Had she been too passionate for Stephen, too eager? It had seemed so natural then. When he tried to unfasten her dress and could not manage the hooks she had helped him; when he took off his clothes she could not help staring.

'Why do you look at me like that?'

'I've never seen a man naked before, not a white man.'

'Are they any different?'

She was not going to say so, but a naked white man seemed much more naked than a naked Indian. She stared so doubtfully at Stephen that he laughed.

'Don't you like it?'

'Some of it,' said Rosa doubtfully.

It was not easy, and Stephen had hurt her, he had been hard with her there on the bed in that room of moon and shadows; but when it was over he had been so gentle and humble that she could not believe he had been cruel.

'Did I hurt you, my little love? I meant to be so gentle.'

Rosa, humble too, had told him to hurt her.

'Then you liked it? Oh Rosa!'

'I can get to like it,' said Rosa. She lay back on the pillow and played with his hair; he looked like a wild boy lying there in the moon with no clothes on and his hair over his eyes. 'You look like a boy who is wild and will never grow up.'

'Mowgli or Peter Pan or both?'

'Who are Mowgli and Peter Pan?'

Rosa could find nothing in any of that to make Stephen angry.

Perhaps he was afraid, afraid of what he had done, that she would make him pay as Belle had made Mr Harman. He need not have been afraid, and sharply on that thought, she knew why he had not come. It was his promise . . .

'If we decide to love each other I shall marry you before we do – or immediately after.'

Decide! They had not decided, they had simply been overtaken by something stronger than themselves. Rosa stood twisting her hands by the typewriter, not knowing what to do.

She had dreamed and wanted with all her heart that Stephen should marry her; she had built a hundred hopes on his promise, but more than that she wanted to see him again. 'If he didn't want to marry me would I make him?' she whispered. 'Oh Stephen, why should you think that of me?'

She knew that she loved him far more than he could ever love her, even though it was he who had done all the loving, all the talking; and yet however she reasoned and talked to herself, she had never been able to give up this silly persistent hope that he would love her and marry her. After all, it had happened with two people like themselves, sometimes the man loved the girl enough to marry her and then he had been dismissed from his firm and they had gone away to England. 'But if he can't keep his promise, I shall love him just the same. Even if he *won't* keep it, if only I could write to him and tell him not to be afraid.'

Her fingers went over the keys, tapping out nonsense, tapping out 'if we decide, if we decide', which was nonsense. There was no other noise in the house, only Blanche sometimes calling out, for she was restless again in the heat. They had lifted her bed away from the wall and the cracks in the plaster were spreading.

The wind rose suddenly, slamming the shutters, swirling dust and leaves and rubbish across the lawn; the crows were shaken from the trees and a dead palm-leaf fell with a crash and rattle on the grass; there was a smell of rain and presently it came, in blots, and then a deluge, driving in strong straight lines into the earth.

People ran to the windows and doors to look at the rain as if a spring had released them; the children began to bother if they might paddle in the drains. Blanche asked for a blanket and then if she might have some cheese to eat; she was given some of her expensive arrowroot and fell asleep with her cheek on her hand.

'She is better,' said auntie, and went to sit on the veranda, her knees apart, her feet turned up on a stool to catch the damp coolness.

In the first days of rain there were never enough umbrellas. Coolies ran down the street holding a cloth over their heads, some held wicker shields and bent themselves double to keep themselves dry. Boy wrapped a sack round his shoulders when he went to fetch the stores. It was good to be wet; the people in the street chattered joyfully, the rickshaws and taxis and carriages splashed up and down with the rain coming through and under their hoods.

Only Rosa looked dully out on the rain; she stood by the window in the bedroom leaning her head against the wire netting; she had put away the typewriter, she could do nothing but think miserably of Stephen.

There was a chink and scattering of plaster that made her look round: a piece had fallen away from the wall where Blanche's bed had been and, as she looked, a great patch fell and crumbled.

Every year when the rains came, the plaster in that one place would not hold, every year they built it up and washed over the stains with distemper, and father said, 'You should leave it, all that plaster and damp will bring the whole wall away,' and now the plaster had fallen and some of the bricking had come away with it, for it had left a deep place in the wall.

Rosa went to see; father was right, the bricking was crumbling and loose, and it came away in her fingers. It was not brick at all, but something powdery, and suddenly her fingers found an edge, hard as stone, running across the wall; it was like the edge of a picture frame, ridged, and as she chipped she saw it dull white under the red powder. Her fingers were getting sore; she took off her shoe and knocked it on the wall, the plaster split into segments and some fell on the floor. She went into the pantry to find something to scrape with. 'A spoon, not too sharp, there's something under the brick and I don't want to scratch it.' She took a wooden spoon.

There was another edge running down to meet the first, making a corner, and between the edges a carving began to appear; not exactly a carving, not exactly a modelling, something in relief on the wall, swelling into curves and hollows.

She uncovered it, little by little; a curve going up, some feathery lines and the paws of an animal set together; its back, and here was its tail, thick and plumy, pressed against its back.

'I believe—' breathed Rosa and quickly she followed the lines, tapping up for the head and scraping away the background so that it showed more clearly.

Blanche woke, for someone was pushing her bed, turning her round to face the wall.

'Why must you—' she began pettishly, and her voice died away.

There on the wall, the wall she had slept under every night, among the cracks and broken plaster, a little dog in stone on the wall, sitting with his back pressed against a ridged edge so that his tail was spread up on his back. He was looking up with round eyes, he was stained and discoloured from the plaster, with dust in his cracks, but still plump, still curly, still cheerful.

'Rosa!' cried Blanche, beginning to gasp and whimper, for she was very weak, 'Oh Rosa, it's Echo!'

'I thought it might be,' said Rosa.

# 15

Her writing was spiky like Janet's and she wrote on flimsy paper that had been made wet by the rain; it felt to Stephen like the petal of a flower.

DEAR STEPHEN,

I hope you are well. I am writing to tell you something to interest you, I think it is interesting. The rain brought down a peice of our wall, I think it is a tabblet put up in memory of someone dead, but I have only uncovered a little peice which is a dog. I didn't tell you before that I have seen a lady here who is a ghost, well this is her dog. Blanche has seen him often before. You can see him quite planely. It is rather funny, isn't it? Please Stephen come as you have always come.

Your friend,

ROSA LEMARCHANT

Stephen had the letter on his desk, leaning on his elbows, and read it again. He did not understand about the lady who was a ghost and the dog, but he understood the last words, 'Please Stephen come as you have always come,' and he knew that Rosa was trying to tell him that she did not mean him to keep his promise. The tight rein that had been choking him was gone, the feeling of panic, and again he saw her still small face; in the garden where they had walked under the palms in jasmine scent and fireflies, on the bed, her eyes shut, spent against the pillow; 'I can get to like it,' and 'Who is Peter Pan?'

'*Burra Sahib salaam detha*,' said a patient voice at his elbow, and William came by and said, 'Tommy wants you in his room.'

'Have you been talking to him?' asked Stephen quickly. 'If you have I'll—'

'Go and see,' said William, 'don't keep him waiting, he doesn't like it.'

Stephen picked up the pamphlet on Soldo Lead that he was working on, and went through to Sir Thomas's room.

'Stephen, I'm an old friend of your father's.'

'Oh, Christ!' thought Stephen, and blushed to the tips of his ears; in his hands he twisted and turned the pamphlet on Soldo Lead.

Sir Thomas was true to type; he said all the things that Stephen so often had imagined he would say, that he knew them almost by heart; but they had a new force coming from Tommy, and, had he said them yesterday, Stephen would have hailed them with relief; now with Rosa's letter on his desk, he felt as if he were being driven into a corner. He refused and set his teeth.

'Packet of trouble – run into debt – these girls very fascinating, I know – your mother—' rumbled Sir Thomas and then asked with startling directness: 'What do you think yourself?'

'I think you've been talking to William,' said Stephen distantly.

'I've been using my eyes and my ears,' said Sir Thomas sharply, 'and I warn you—'

'Well, how was he?' asked William when Stephen came out. 'What did he say?'

'What you meant him to. God, what a muck heap this place is. Doesn't matter what you do if you're not serious, or what filth you commit to save your face.'

'Calcutta code,' said William pleasantly. 'You conform or go.'

'Then I'll bloody well go.'

'We had a donkey when we were children,' said William. 'Doubtless you remember him, Raphael was his name, and the only way to make him go was to try and ride him in the opposite direction.'

'Well, what would you do?'

'That rather depends,' answered William, 'on what you have done.'

The peon brought Stephen's note to Rosa, the same that had brought all his notes, a peon in a khaki shirt and a brass disc with C & C on it, and an umbrella hooked into the back of his collar.

I'll come after tea. Love, Stephen. I want you to have this!

It was a cheque for a hundred rupees.

Rosa tapped the letter thoughtfully against her thumb; she wondered what had happened to her that she understood Stephen so exactly, that she suddenly had become grown-up and wise.

'Is he coming?' asked Blanche. 'Oh, he is! Well, I want Robert to come too.'

'He can't come in here,' said Rosa quickly.

'He can, if Stephen can. I want Robert.'

'What makes you say that now? I thought you were fond of Stephen?'

'I am when he's here,' said Blanche slowly. 'That's the funny thing, Rosa. When Stephen is here I think he's like an angel, and when he isn't he reminds me more of the devil.'

'Blanche! You who talked so much of his being an angel. You're so fickle!'

'Not at all,' said Blanche. 'And the devil was an angel first, remember.'

'Who told you to give me this cheque?' Rosa asked Stephen when he came.

'No one,' he lied. 'Why?'

'Someone told you. Who was it?'

'You've grown very wise,' said Stephen. 'As a matter of fact it was William.'

William had said: 'How much did you send her? A hundred rupees. Expensive! The rate is twenty.' Stephen hated him for that.

'So you talk about me to William?'

'Certainly I do. Is that a crime?'

'This is a crime between us,' said Rosa, holding out the cheque. 'You give me a hundred rupees because I – loved you. Thank you. I won't take money for that. I won't take money from you.'

'Oh, won't you?' said Stephen cruelly. 'How ridiculous you are! You won't take it openly and honestly. You'll borrow and forget to pay it back, all the whole pack of you, but if I say it's given, you're insulted. That's how you cheat yourself, if you do cheat yourself.'

Rosa had turned her back upon him; only her shoulders moved, bowed and quivering as if he had struck her on the breast. Outside the rain had stopped, the clouds had parted, there was a green sky left from the sunset and one star in the window frame. Rosa kept her eyes on that star: it glimmered and winked in the tears she would not let Stephen see; the cheque lay on the floor behind her.

'Rosa,' he said, in another voice. 'Rosa, I've been saying terrible things. Things I never meant to say. I've been so worried and miserable. It's my bloody temper. Oh Rosa, turn round. Let me see. Look at me. Oh! I've made you cry.'

'Not the first tears Stephen, not the last,' but she let him wipe them away with his handkerchief, for the sake of being in his arms.

'How ridiculous you are,' Stephen said again, but the sting had gone out of the words.

'Why do you stay *talking*?' called Blanche through the partition. 'Stephen, don't talk. Come and see who's here.'

When they had gone into Blanche and only the star was left shining into the empty room, father came in from the veranda on tip-toe, and picked up the cheque and put it in his pocket.

# 16

'You must ask before you take down the wall,' cried auntie. 'You must ask Mr deSouza. You know very well, Rosa, what trouble we had when we built out the doolie. What damages he wanted us to pay! You must ask Mr deSouza.'

'I'll ask him,' said Stephen blithely. 'Where is he?'

It was the first time he had been in the house except in the vestibule where the ceiling was so far away that the colours were blurred into a green yellow and the shapes lost. Now he stayed on the top step to look at it, and eagerly he sensed the strangeness of those landings, where the new impressions fought against the impervious old delicate days. 'I wonder if they'd let me go all through the house,' he whispered. 'I'm getting nearer. I can feel it. Things are happening fast.' He looked up again at those riders chasing past the wooded trees, the hounds leaping to the stag, and he seemed to hear the galloping down the dale and the stirring note of a horn.

Mr deSouza was in his shirt sleeves, reading the paper and picking his teeth with a quill pick; the zircon flashed on his little finger as he lifted his hand. At a long table the children were having supper. The big ones continued to eat slices of pineapple, but the little ones put down their spoons to gaze at Stephen, whom Blanche had often described to them as an angel; and indeed, he was all in white, with yellow hair, he only needed wings and to take off his socks and shoes. Robert stood up and went to lean against the window, picking his teeth too, but his were small and unbroken like a child's and shining white against his olive skin.

'He's marvellously good-looking,' thought Stephen, 'in a technicolour way. All of them are, except the old man. What a gorgeous stone.' He had not seen a zircon, and thought it was a blue diamond.

'And what can I do for you?' said Mr deSouza. Stephen explained what they wanted.

'But I do not wish,' said Mr deSouza, 'to have the wall structurally altered.'

'It can't hurt the wall, it's only a question of removing the plaster and a wash of brick powder. We might discover something of great historical importance.'

'Then I should like to discover it myself.'

'Well, come and do it, then,' cried Stephen.

'Mr Bright, I am a very busy man,' said Mr deSouza with dignity. 'I have not many moments, Mr Bright.'

'Then let me do it. I'll pay for it. What more do you want? I have told you it may be an important discovery, historically very important.' But the more Stephen talked of important historical discoveries the more anxious seemed Mr deSouza to prevent them.

Stephen grew desperate. 'I have to tell you,' he said, 'I should have told you before, that I have already discovered a curious thing in your garden, a sundial, Mr deSouza.' And remembering, he explained: 'A sun clock dating back to the end of the eigh-teenth century, 1790 to be exact, and what is more curious, it bears the same motto and emblem as the famous old French tapestries in the Cluny Museum in Paris, called "The Lady and the Unicorn".'

Robert had taken a step towards Stephen. His face was vivid with interest. 'And I can tell you—' he began, when Mr deSouza held up his hand.

'You have no business,' he said, 'to discover a thing like that in my garden, on my property.'

'But don't you *see*,' groaned Stephen, 'how it will increase the value of your property? I think the wing you have let to the Lemarchants must once have been a chapel, by the formation of the windows and the niche; now we have found this tablet I am *certain* it was a chapel. A tremendous amount of interest would be aroused by that and would attach itself to the house.'

'Tcha! That is the last thing I could wish,' cried Mr deSouza. 'Promise me you will say nothing of this to anyone.'

'But *why?*'

'This is a private house and I will not have people spying in here on my property. It will upset – my wife, who is delicate. It would upset my tenants. No, no, Mr Bright, you will please leave it alone. You must promise me not to say any word to anyone.'

'But why?'

'I have my own reasons Mr Bright. After all, you must allow me that the property is mine. You can't dictate to me. I must have your promise.'

'If I promise, will you let me break down the wall?'

'No, no. That I cannot do.'

'Then I shall write to the *Statesman*,' said Stephen firmly, 'and tell them all that I have found and suspect.'

Mr deSouza looked at Stephen and Stephen looked back at Mr deSouza, who tapped with his tooth-pick on the table; the zircon, like another eye, clearly blue, watched Stephen.

'Mr Bright,' he said, 'I'll tell you what I will do. You will pay for everything, and you will solemnly give me your promise not to show it or tell it to anyone, and you must see that the Lemarchants don't either, for I don't trust them at all; and then you may carefully take down that one piece of plaster on the wall.'

'Thank you very much!' said Stephen dryly.

Auntie did not like Stephen to come into the bedroom. She felt shy, and snatched up a hairbrush full of wisps of grey hair and shut it in a drawer; but he was so excited that he scarcely knew it was a bedroom, and pushed the beds out of the way, and put his tools down on the chest-of-drawers, without thinking of what he was doing.

It took him two days to uncover the tablet; he had to work delicately and moaned that he could get no outside help. 'Why the stupid old fool wants it kept secret!' he said. 'This should be done by experts.' And Rosa kept quiet, remembering how she had scraped and hacked where Stephen worked so delicately.

Slowly the plaster and bricking came away, and he asked Rosa to bring a brush and carefully wash off the last traces.

'I'll tell Boy,' she said.

'Can't you do it?' asked Stephen.

'I scrub and brush? I'm not a servant,' said Rosa.

'Good Lord!' cried Stephen impatiently. 'All right, I'll do it myself. Tell Boy to leave the things here.'

They gathered round him as he cleaned it, Rosa, auntie, father, Boy, and Blanche watching from her bed.

It was a memorial tablet and the lettering was still plainly seen. Above it was a scroll with a wreath and two weeping cherubs, below, to the right, Echo looked up at the inscription, and to the left a unicorn, like a horse with low legs and the horn running up from its forehead, bore against its shoulders a shield with three crescent moons.

Consecrated to the memory of Rosabelle (née LeViste) for one day the wife of Joseph Paul Lemarchant, who died on the evening of her wedding day, 12th October, 1792, aged seventeen years and is buried, innocent and virgin, in this foreign land.

Erected by her husband in grief too deep to express in the Name of her blessed Redeemer and the hope of her forgiveness.

Stephen read the words aloud, and there was a silence when his voice ceased. They gazed reverently at the tablet; only auntie's lips moved: she was praying.

'Rosabelle Lemarchant,' breathed Rosa; 'my name and Belle's joined together, and we are twins. Oh, Stephen! We must be descended from her. We must be!'

'We are,' said father. 'I always knew it. You hear that, Anna?' But auntie had gone out. She was sad to think they had that tablet in their room. 'We are descended from her,' repeated father.

'You can't be descended from a virgin,' said Stephen crushingly.

Rosa's face clouded. Over and over again she read the name that was hers and Belle's as if searching for some hidden meaning. 'Oh, I wish Belle were here, I wish she'd known. This must be something to do with us.'

'What is that?' asked Blanche, pointing to the unicorn.

'It's a unicorn,' said Stephen.

'Is it real, like Echo?' asked Blanche doubtfully.

'No. It must have been a crest or an emblem, part of her coat-of-arms. The animals over your windows are meant to be unicorns, too, I think; and the one on the sundial. It must have been the Lady Rosabelle's signet.'

'But Echo isn't a signet,' said Blanche indignantly, 'he's real. I've seen him. I met him in the passage just before I got sick. I'm glad,' she added, 'I'm glad it wasn't the unicorn I met in the passage, Stephen.'

All the same, the unicorn was rather sweet, with his little low hooves and great eyes and the horn in the middle of his forehead.

'What colour could he be, Stephen?'

'White as milk with blue, blue shadows in his shadowy parts.'

'And his horn?'

'Like a shell, not pink nor yellow, but in between.'

'But Echo is sweeter,' said jealous Blanche.

'Echo is quite different,' said Stephen gravely, 'he's a Person.'

Rosa was reading over the words on the tablet.

'Her name *is* Belle's and mine joined together. Stop talking to Blanche, Stephen, and think. It must mean something. Why should she have the same name?'

'It may be pure coincidence,' said Stephen, 'but it's very extraordinary. There may be something in it.'

Already at the thought the blood in Rosa, in all of them, seemed to flower as if it flowed strongly from an old strong source.

'I believe in it,' she said obstinately. 'She was my great-great-great-grandmother, or if she can't be that she was my great-great-great-aunt. I haven't worked out how many greats.' She was like an old-time Chinese before the tablets of his ancestors. 'Why else do I feel for her so? I feel as if she were my sister, as if she were Blanche or Belle and I had grown up with her all my life. I am as sorry as if she had died to-day. Oh, I wonder what she was like.'

'I think she was like you,' said Stephen suddenly.

'Like me! Oh Stephen. I believe you're right.'

'Like you when you use your hands so much for talking, and the way you speak, too quickly to be English; and your eyes and hair so dark, and your skin so curiously white, not like a northern skin. You might be a foreigner, and you have that heart-broken expression just as she had, I think, when she was left here in this foreign place, "buried in this foreign land, aged seventeen years",' he quoted.

'It sounds so sorry,' said Blanche.

'It is,' said Stephen. '"Erected by her husband in the hope of her forgiveness". What did he do to her, I wonder? I wonder if he built this chapel to her memory and that's why it has her emblem over the windows? The shield for her name, the uni-corn for her maidenhood. The natives couldn't model the unicorn very well, that's why it puzzled us. This one was done by an artist, it's beautiful. Perhaps Joseph Paul bricked up the sun-dial because it reminded him too much of her; she must have brought it from France, from her old home perhaps, to save it from the revolution, perhaps her home was sabotaged. That would explain it and the chapel.'

'No, the chapel was here first, before she died,' said Rosa. 'I saw her, Stephen, she ran to the chapel, and auntie saw her too, she saw her fall on her knees there; you see, she has made her table into an altar, where the altar was.

'Her father went away,' said Rosa softly as if she were speaking in a dream. 'I think he must have been her father, for his hair was white and she loved him very much, he went away in the early morning before it was light; the servants carried down his luggage and they were tired, they had been up all night, for I think there was a ball; yes, Robert thought he heard music. Rosabelle had on a dress of blue silk, bright like a purple-blue flower, and at the last she couldn't help weeping, pleading with him not to leave her.'

'Was she married then?' interrupted Stephen.

'I don't know. I think she was, he wouldn't have left her if she weren't, would he? He didn't want to leave her then, but he put her away from him and told her to go upstairs. As the wheels rolled away she tried to run after him, then turned to the pillar and wept. She heard someone coming to find her, steps coming down the stairs, a man's steps that she hated, and she ran to hide herself where he couldn't find her; she ran to the chapel to fall on her knees by the altar. She ran and then Belle came—'

'*Belle* came? What do you mean?'

'Belle came,' repeated Rosa, like someone in a dream, and then seemed to waken with a start, and cried, 'Oh, Stephen, that girl's face when she heard the man's steps coming down the stairs! I wonder if she killed herself that night. Oh, she was so unhappy, Stephen. When she heard him coming she couldn't bear it. She was afraid. She hated him. I'm glad she died before he took her. Oh, I'm glad she died before that.'

# 17

Stephen came with such excitement that he could hardly speak.

'Rosa, look. Just look. Here is the book that Janet sent from the Cluny Museum. You know, I told you, the museum where those tapestries are, the Cluny in Paris. It must be the best authority, it's by Marquet de Vasselot, the keeper of the Museums, the Cluny and the Louvre. He says here – wait till I find it – he says: 'The armorial bearings upon the banners and pennants are the full arms of the LeViste family, a great family of Lyon.' Now turn to the illustrations, to the banners and pennants, and you'll see they're the same, three crescent moons on a crossway strip: the same as the shields on the sundial and windows and the banner on the tablet, the very same. Don't you see that it means this must be the LeViste family of the tapestries? It definitely establishes it. God! this is going to make a sensation when I'm ready to tell it.'

'You can't tell it,' said Rosa; 'you gave your promise to Mr deSouza.'

The light faded from Stephen's face, it was blank with dismay. 'He'll have to let me take it back, he'll release me from it. He'll

139

have to, in a case like this. It's not one man's right, it's – it's a
world right – I'm going to ask him now.'

'You can't ask him – he's gone to Bombay.'

'Can't Robert?'

'Robert would say "No" . . .'

'You mean because he's jealous.'

'He's jealous of you, and besides he's jealous of my finding
this – this connection of our family with the Le Viste family, and
now you say they are great he'll be more jealous still.'

'Good God, how petty! Can't he think of it in a wider sense?
Can't you? No, I don't think you can. All that it means to you
is that you might possibly be connected with a great family . . .'

Rosa was not listening. She was turning over the pages, written half in French and half in English, drinking them in with
delight.

The six pieces which compose this famous set of tapestries
adorned at one time the Castle of Boussac in the Creuse.
This Castle was bought in 1837 by the City . . . who sold the
tapestries to the Cluny Museum in 1882 . . . The artist has
limited the blue ground to a sort of island in which he has
confined each of his scenes; and in each case he has
detached this principal part on a rose-coloured background,
scattered also with plants, flowers and small animals . . .
Each of the pieces shows a young woman elegantly arrayed,
accompanied by heraldic animals, a lion and a unicorn,
both carrying banners and pennants covered with the same
armorial bearings. These arms belonged to a family called
Le Viste. This family was related to different houses in
Provence and in Dauphiné and gave a president to the
Parliament of Paris. A member of this family in the time of

Charles VIII or Louis XII ordered this set of tapestries of which six have come down to us ... five of these pieces of tapestries composed without doubt an allegorical representation of the five senses, while the sixth of different arrangement and more ample proportion had another meaning. For five of these pieces the explanation is ingenious and we should accept it; but with regard to the sixth we are not quite satisfied. Why is this last surmounted by the inscription MON SEUL DÉSIR? If this 'desire' applies to the jewel handled by the Lady it might denote a glorification of coquettishness and the whole series would thus have a realistic and worldly meaning. But could not this be a motto? ... the bearings upon the banners and pennants are the full arms of the LeViste family and a married woman would not have the right to exhibit such arms unless she belonged by descent to the same family as her husband. If these arms are those of the Lady represented, she therefore would rather be an unmarried woman ... according to ... researches the Cluny tapestries would have been made for Claude LeViste, daughter of Jean LeViste Lord of Arcy and President of the *Cour Des Aides*, and of Geneviève of Nanterre; they would have been woven between 1509 and 1513 ...

'1513,' Rosa looked up at Stephen. 'That's more than two hundred years before Rosabelle.'

'Two hundred years is not very long in the history of a family like that. It makes it more probable. Think of the hundreds of off-shoots they must collect, cousins of cousins and second cousins.'

Read Rosa:

'Claude LeViste, daughter of Jean LeViste and Geneviève of Nanterre. A further remark would rather seem to strengthen this theory. Everyone knows that the unicorn is one of the symbols of virginity. It was believed during the middle ages ... that this fantastic beast could not be captured unless a young girl attracted it and lulled it to sleep on her lap.'

She turned to the illustrations of the six tapestries:

### SIGHT

The Lady sitting, holds with her right hand the mirror up to the unicorn, which kneels with its front hooves laid on her lap.

### HEARING

The Lady standing, plays a small portable organ which is placed upon a high table covered by a carpet; on the other side of the table a waiting-maid standing, works the bellows of the organ.

### SMELL

The Lady standing, holds in her two hands a crown of flowers; before her stands a young waiting-maid holding a gilt platter containing flowers; behind her a small monkey is playing with flowers placed in a basket upon a stool.

### FEELING

The Lady standing, caresses with her left hand the horn of the unicorn standing beside her; with her right hand she holds the staff of a banner with armorial bearings.

TASTE

The Lady standing, takes with the right hand a sweetmeat from a gilt cup presented to her by a young waiting-maid, on her left hand is perched a small parrot, which shows its greedy impatience by flapping its wings.

MON SEUL DÉSIR

The Lady standing in front of a tent which is held open on one side by the lion and on the other side by the unicorn, takes a gold chain from the casket held by a young waiting-maid. Across the top of the tent is inscribed in capitals: – À ... MON ... SEUL ... DÉSIR ... ?

'The jewel handled by the Lady,' said Stephen, 'I wonder if that's a clue.'

'Clue to what?' asked Rosa.

'Now let me think,' said Stephen, straddling a chair and resting his chin on the back of it. 'Why should anyone in their senses bring a sundial all the way from France to Bengal? A ready-cast dial, remember, that couldn't possibly work in such a different latitude.'

'You said it was to remind her of her garden at home.'

'Yes, and that seems to me a pawky reason. I think there was something hidden in it, something the Revolution might take, a family heirloom. In the morning as soon as it's light, I'm coming down and I'm going over that sundial with a toothcomb.'

'Do you really think you'll find something?'

'I might. It's worth trying. Why didn't I think of it before?'

Rosa, looking more intently at the illustration cried, 'Oh, Blanche! I must show this to Blanche; look, Stephen, on the cushion, the little dog: it's Echo again.'

It was Echo, sitting on the brocaded cushion under the canopy of the Lady's veil; unawed by the lion and the unicorn, the small Echo gazed calmly out through the centuries on the world.

'It's too extraordinary,' breathed Stephen. 'What can it mean? Show it to Blanche, Rosa, and see what she says.'

Blanche was reading the leaflet of a worm powder for big and little dogs, and seemed not at all surprised to see Echo in the tapestry.

'What kind of a dog would you say he was, Stephen?'

'Well, I should think – only I don't know what they called him then – I should think he was a little spaniel. Now I wonder if he came from Spain, and that was why they called him Echo.'

'Echo is his name,' said Blanche, 'and I don't think he's very like a spaniel.'

'Nowadays he would be called a King Charles spaniel.'

'King Charles spaniel … I never thought of that,' said Blanche. 'Thank you, Stephen.'

# 18

When auntie heard that their suite was a chapel, she felt uncomfortable; she could not bring herself to sit alone now except on the veranda, and even if Joseph and the children were there, she sat on the edge of her chair and felt she must whisper; and how apologetic she was when she ate and slept almost where the altar had been; she would have moved her bed away from her table, but there was no other place for it. She shut away her pin-tray and her jewel-box in a drawer and put her crucifix on the table with a clean napkin under it.

'Why do you mind?' asked Blanche, up for the first time in the sitting-room. 'It's just the same as it was before.'

'I think,' whispered auntie, 'that I should put away that photograph of Belle when she was a baby in her singlet, don't you?'

'I don't see why,' said Blanche. 'In some of the holy pictures Jesus has no clothes at all, only a halo, and you can't count a halo, can you? Belle at any rate has a vest.'

'Well, yes, she has.' Auntie was a little comforted. 'But you should say Our Lord Jesus Christ, Blanche, and bow your head.'

Now Stephen came in for early morning tea. That was too

much, auntie thought, with none of them up, and auntie in her curlers. Rosa would not tell her what they had been doing, but it was something to do with the sundial.

'It couldn't be buried under it,' said Stephen, 'they must have brought it in the sundial or there was no sense in bringing it at all, but I can't find a trace. I can't believe they brought the whole thing, the pedestal and plinth, it must weigh a ton, besides, it's so crudely made; so that leaves the dial. There must be some sort of attachment underneath it I should think. It's all in one piece and the style is welded with it. We'll have to take the dial right out.'

Every morning as soon as it was light Stephen came with a drill that a native mason had taught him to use; slowly he drilled round the dial, separating it from the stone, and always before he went away he covered it with the jasmine, and no one knew what he was doing but Rosa; Blanche, who found out everything, was in bed. When he had drilled right round the face they found that still they could not lift the dial.

'It's sunk in putty or cement or some such,' groaned Stephen. 'I shall have to drill right underneath.'

He began again the weary hours of drilling; Rosa was tired of it, especially as Stephen would not tell her what he hoped to find, but he was endlessly patient. At last one day he found that he could lift the dial a little at the sides.

'Give it a good heave,' suggested Rosa.

'My dear girl, in a thing like this you have to work very delicately. There might be a spring that might get broken.'

Day after day he went on until very carefully and deliberately, he could lift the dial from its bed of stone and, scarcely breathing with excitement, with careful steady hands they lifted it out.

There was nothing there; the underside when they had

cleaned it was as bare and smooth as a worn copper coin, there was no trace of a hiding place or a spring. Stephen turned it over and over; the only markings were the grooves that divided the hours, and curiously, they were marked on the bottom as well. Stephen ran his thumb nail along them, but there was no difference between them, they were all the same indented line.

They scraped away the softer stone until the top of the pedestal appeared. Stephen shook his head. He looked ready to cry with disappointment. 'There's nothing here. Well, well. That comes of having a too fervent imagination.'

'What did you expect to find?'

'I thought it might be jewels, they'd hardly put money in a place like that. Something they wanted to smuggle out of the country; it was a year of the French Revolution, remember. A diamond necklace, or pearls or something.'

'Oh, if it had been!' sighed Rosa. 'It would have belonged to us.'

'I suppose you'd have had as good a right as anyone.'

'Would they have been worth a lot of money, Stephen?'

'Well, they'd hardly have gone to all that trouble if they weren't. Still, there's nothing there and that's that. Now I suppose I've got to put all this back.'

Auntie wished they had never found the tablet; nothing was the same since they had discovered it, with Stephen in and out of the bedroom and Robert quarrelling with Rosa, and Rosa saying she was a lady, and Blanche talking your sense away with Echo this and Echo that.

Now they were looking in the old cemeteries for the graves of the Lemarchants. Father, who would not go and lay as much as a four-anna lily on his own wife's grave, went in the rain and heat to search the records with Stephen and Rosa; for now father was sure he was the direct descendant of that Joseph Lemarchant; he said he remembered hearing it from his mother.

It was exhausting in that hot and rainy weather, and soon father's pain came on and he left the search to the others. They went in the evenings when the rain had stopped; the ground hissed and steamed like a kettle, and there was a cold earthen smell among the graves that clung to hands and clothes where they had touched them.

'I shall hate dying after this,' said Stephen. 'I shall be cremated.' Rosa was shocked, for she had been taught that it was beautiful and important to have a headstone or a marble cross, with as many wreaths as possible.

The moss and the fungus, the young dead people and the weeping trees depressed them, filled them with a nervous melancholy; Stephen would have given up but for Rosa's insistence. It was strange for Rosa to give Stephen orders; she even dared to nag him.

'We must find them, Stephen, we must.'

'We've searched the South Cemetery and the North Cemetery. St John's is too early, the Circular Road one too late. They're not in the records. So what?'

'But there are graves, and stones not mentioned in the records. I shall *die* if we can't find *anything*.'

'It seems as if you'll have to die, then,' said Stephen unsympathetically. He was sick of this endless searching in the wet and dirt. 'They must have been obliterated or built over if ever they were here. For all we know none of them died here.'

'We know Rosabelle died here.'

They were standing in the porch beside the North Cemetery gate, for the rain had begun again and was beating down on the path, on the mournful iron gates, and the road beyond where the car was waiting. The porch, with its shields and tablets, was empty except for the gatekeeper who had long ago ceased to take an interest in Rosa and Stephen; he came in and out from his house, emptying a pot of water, fetching a bundle of sticks that were drying beside a brazier that made a fume of charcoal smoke on the damp air. He came out from his house again and twitched down a cloth that had been hung to dry on the wall; where it had hung was a plaque of old iron, lettered in white and level with the wall.

'How did we miss that?' cried Stephen, drawing Rosa across the porch. Standing together, hand in hand, they read the inscription; spelling it out, letter by letter, for it was far more worn than the tablet in the chapel, and as they read Rosa clutched his hand, digging her nails in, in her excitement. 'It is. It is,' she breathed.

Sacred to the memory of Claude-Marie (née LeViste) beloved wife of Joseph Lemarchant, Merchant of the East India Company, obit 9th April 1799, leaving her infant children to mourn her in the pious hope of joyful resurrection.

Beloved for Honour, Spirit, Sense and Truth,
To memory sacred. Worth's unfading ray
Is fondly cherished to our closing day,
In hope that an equal course maintain
Blest be us all when we shall meet again.

Also to the memory of Joseph Paul Lemarchant a Senior Merchant of the East India Company, who departed this transitory life 21st July 1817. This tablet was inscribed with his name at his own request.

'I told you so,' said Rosa, standing before it while the rain drove in round her shoulders. 'I knew it was true. It couldn't happen and mean nothing, nothing at all. Now will you believe me, Stephen, when I tell you that the girl, the ghost we say, might have been me? Oh, you must see her, Stephen. We must sit up and wait. This one, "Claude-Marie", it is from her we are ,descended, but I have no feeling for her as I have for Rosabelle. You must see her Stephen, my great-great- what?' She paused uncertainly. 'Aunt, I think, they must have been sisters. We'll sit up to-night.'

'If you want to know,' said Stephen with a yawn, 'I've sat up four nights running and I haven't seen a blessed thing. Not one single thing. Come out of the rain. Your hair's getting wet.'

'But *I* have seen her, and Robert and Mr Mascarenes, only he has gone, and auntie. I have told you and you know—'

'You have told me and I know, that Robert has seen her and Mr Mascarenes has seen her, and auntie and you, but I have *not* seen her and I don't care who has. It conveys nothing to me whatsoever. Let's go home. I'm tired.'

Why did Stephen fail to see Rosabelle, 'the Lady' as Robert called her? There seemed no answer to that question and it made Stephen angry. Of all the people concerned, he felt he should have been the one; he began it, and he thought he could say without conceit that he was of them all the most sensitive, the most rare, except that he was not certain about Robert and oddly, Blanche, in the corner of his mind. There was something in Robert and Blanche, but he could only glimpse it, they never let him come near enough to them to see it.

He had spent the whole of one night in a long barren vigil, but he had fallen asleep towards dawn; the next night his bearer woke him at four and he watched until the sun was up, but perhaps he had been too late. After that he stayed up in a party and arrived about three o'clock, and he was not quite sure that he had not been drunk, but there was no doubt about the last night. He was wide-awake and sober, and spent the hours from one till five sitting on the steps of the porch or stairs, changing his position every few minutes, walking on the edge of the drive, or pacing the vestibule.

It was the night for a ghost, dark and full of sounds, and the palms, like voices, endlessly whispered in the darkness. A twig dropped, Stephen swung round on his heel; a cat ran across the gravel almost at his feet and sent the blood racing into his face.

When the dawn came into the garden, slowly brimming it with light, he knew that the night was over and he had seen nothing again. He ached and shivered from sitting on the stones, his eyes felt hot and strained, and he was tired and angry. In the rain-soaked garden the light shone on the lawn and the stiff-fingered palm-leaves; two birds like wrens were hopping round the olean-der bushes, there was a wind, young, fresh and cheerful.

A Chinaman stopped in the road and put his black-bristled head through the door that Stephen had left open. 'You buy?' he asked, though he knew it was improbable. 'Good morning. Velly nice day. You buy?'

Mr deSouza came back from Bombay and Stephen laid siege to him, but he would not give in. Stephen argued and prayed and threatened, but it was of no use, Mr deSouza grew tired of seeing him and hid when the children said he was coming. At last one day when Stephen had been talking until Mr deSouza was desperate, he held up his hand and cried: 'Stop, Mr Bright, stop. I ask you to stop. Now, I will make a bargain with you. You will go away and worry me no more, and after, let us say, the first of December, you may tell what you like.'

'But that is nearly five months off.'

'Exactly.'

'Why the first of December?' said Stephen suspiciously. 'What is happening? Have you sold the house?'

'This property, Mr Bright, has been in my family for sixty years.'

'Yes, but you've sold it now, haven't you?'

'I may have. I don't know.'

'I couldn't make him say anything more,' Stephen told Rosa, 'but I am sure he's sold it.'

'I don't mind if he has,' said Rosa. 'It would be nicer here without him and Robert.'

'If only he'd be *reasonable*,' chafed Stephen. 'To think that I can't even tell William and Gray.'

'I don't understand you,' said Rosa in a hard voice, 'you keep your promise to him even when you are tempted, even when it seems unreasonable, but—'

She broke off, horrified. She had nearly said what, for a long time she had told herself, she must not say; it was always between them, always uppermost in her mind and in Stephen's, and he now was silent.

It was a long time before he came again. He could not lose the tiredness of those four nights of waiting; he was half dead with fatigue and stifled in the steamy heavy air. His sun-tan had gone, his face was a wax colour tinged with yellow that did not go well with his hair.

'You are not half as pretty as you were,' Blanche said, and, absurdly, that hurt him.

They were on his nerves, they irritated him, especially Rosa. Since they had found the tablet and Claude-Marie's memorial plaque, she had grown as many plumes as Echo's tail, and

Stephen had always that feeling of guilt no matter whether he was with her or whether he was away. Sometimes he could not bear touching her, and again he could not wait to have her; would whisper hoarsely: 'Rosa, you must come with me, now at once. I can't wait,' and then, when he had her in the house, often it would die as suddenly as it came, and he would have to think of an excuse to send her home.

Rosa clung to him, she could not help it, for she was afraid; she who had been unconsciously wise before, now, on the point of her danger, was afraid and clung to Stephen. When he hurt her she cried and sulked, but even her tempers were not exciting for he knew he could break them down in a moment; he had only to smile, and she trembled with pleasure, to say a few words and she broke into chatter. There was nothing new for him to discover, even his interest in the lady, the unicorn and Echo was baulked by Mr deSouza, he could not even see Rosabelle.

The rain seemed to be driving in his head, and Lemarchants, LeVistes, Echo and Rosa, and the words *Mon seul désir*, were always in his mind, irritating, baffling, maddening him.

'Tommy says you're looking ill,' said William in the office. 'Says he'll send you away for a month.'

'Thanks; he can't catch me like that,' said Stephen, and went to see Rosa that night.

Every evening now Rosa put on her new cloque dress and often she came out on the porch to listen, through the rain, for the sound of a car. Robert went away if he saw her, he could not bear to see her there.

She was not looking well either; she had a sallow look when she wanted so much to be attractive. Robert could see how much she tried to make herself attractive by the rouge and the lipstick she put on, that made her look like the painted clay idols they sold in the bazaar, and the way she did up her hair in curls, like a Shirley Temple doll.

Robert often came down to see them now; he was very gentle to Rosa, who was very rude to him; he told stories to Blanche and went on errands for auntie.

'He is a good boy,' said auntie, to whom Robert was still one of the deSouza children; 'he will help me to write my thank-offering, for his writing is so beautiful!'

She had put in the names of all her favourite saints; it would be very expensive, but she was determined to have them all. This was one thing in her life that she would do as she intended, even though she took the five rupees that father had given her for the bazaar.

Robert wrote it out for her:

As promised I publish my thanks to the Sacred Heart of Jesus, Our Mother of Mercy and Good Health, the Little Flower of Jesus, St Philomena, St Juda, St Don Bosco, St Rock, St Thomas More, St Anthony, the Little Rose of China and the Holy Souls in Purgatory for having cured my niece of a serious illness.

ANNA KEMPF

She stood in confusion in the vast vestibule of the Statesman Office in Central Avenue, not knowing which way to go; then she saw a long counter with a notice saying 'Advertisements'.

'This is not an advertisement,' said auntie shyly to the young woman behind the counter. 'I wish to publish my thanks. I am Mrs Kempf, my husband was a German from Germany, and he was a very good photographer. One of his photographs of the

Himalayas won a medal at an exhibition in Europe, and my niece, who is my sister's child, and her name is Blanche Lemarchant, she it is who has been so ill. God knows how she has suffered! At first I thought it was worms—'

'You must fill in this form,' said the young woman patiently, handing a printed form over the counter.

With a trembling hand auntie took it. 'Where do I write?' she asked in a voice like a child, and compared the bewildering form with the sheet of paper where Robert had written out her thank-offering so beautifully.

'Wouldn't this do?' she pleaded, and the young woman took it in the tips of her fingers and read it and relented.

'Put your name and address at the bottom,' she said, 'in the personal column. Front page? You may have to wait, you know.'

'What now?' auntie asked her, but she wisely paid no attention and said: 'That will be five rupees, please.'

'Well, I can borrow the money for the bazaar from Stephen this evening,' said auntie to herself, as she swayed backwards and forwards in the tram. 'Stephen will lend it to me, he said he would come this evening.' She was a little uneasy, but she had made her thank-offering and Stephen was always kind.

She thought of the things she would buy in the bazaar; she would buy them in the same spirit as she had made her thank-offering; for father she would buy smoked hilsa, the fish of which he was always so fond, and a mutton curry to follow it, and for Blanche perhaps at last she would get that carrot juice the doctor talked about, though how you could get juice from a carrot auntie did not know.

She looked round her with a happy smile, and there in the tram was Belle. Auntie was quite embarrassed for Belle to be found in a tram by her aunt with whom she had broken so recently, and wondered if she had better not recognize her, but Belle came at once and sat down beside her.

'Your hat is not straight,' she whispered to auntie, as if they had not parted at all. 'You look very hot. Where have you been?'

'To make my thank-offering for Blanche; she is better.'

Belle nodded absently. It did not matter to her, auntie thought angrily, if her little sister were better or worse. She said spitefully, 'I did not think you were often in a tram nowadays.'

'I'm not,' said Belle calmly. 'Only I have left Mr Harman.'

'*Left* him,' echoed auntie. 'But what will you do now?'

'You needn't worry,' said Belle with a little smile. 'I shall be all right.' Indeed she looked very well; she was thinner but more elegant, wearing a grey suit with orchids and a hat with a veil, she had even a grey umbrella. Auntie longed to ask her two things, how she had left Mr Harman, and if she had paid the doctor.

'I have met somebody else,' said Belle.

'Then why are you in a tram?' asked auntie in shrill surprise.

'Perhaps that is a game I'm playing. At present I haven't very much money, but soon I shall have, I think. What would you say, auntie, if I told you I'm going home to England, and perhaps to America, and that I shall go on the films and be a star? Auntie,' she burst out laughing, 'that is the only way he means me to come back, on the films. You will all be able to look up at me and I shan't see you, for I shall be famous, auntie.'

If it had been one of the others auntie would have said, 'What nonsense you talk, child,' but with Belle she was silent; she had an uncomfortable feeling that it was going to be true, that Belle would be a star on the films. As she talked to auntie she seemed as eager as the charming little girl she once had been, but auntie knew that she was hard and set on her way.

'If he can persuade me,' said Belle, and laughed again.

'*Persuade* you? Don't you want to?'

'Perhaps that is part of the game.' Belle stood up. 'I have to get off here.'

'Rosa wanted to see you,' auntie said unwillingly. 'She wanted to tell you that they have found a tablet in the bedroom. She wanted you to know that you have some old grand relatives through your father, but I think it's shocking, Belle, that our suite should be a chapel—'

Belle was not listening. 'I should like to see Rosa,' she said. 'Tell her to write to me, auntie.'

'You haven't given us your address,' said auntie. 'You went away and didn't tell us. You hurt us very much, Belle.'

Belle stiffened, the hardness came back into her face. 'Give Rosa my love,' she said lightly. 'Tell her she'd better forget me. Good-bye, auntie, good-bye.'

# 19

When auntie came in, eager to tell Rosa that she had seen Belle, she found her walking about the sitting-room, looking from door to window and window to door; she was dressed in her cloque dress, but there were dark rings under her eyes. Belle's news faded from auntie's lips.

'Stephen is late,' she said.

The rain came down with a steady noise for answer; to-night the gutters were full, the folding glass doors had to be shut over the windows, and the rain made an endless small knocking on the pane as if it wanted to be let in. Auntie's feet were drenched in her walk from the tram, all at once she felt very tired.

'Stephen isn't coming,' said Rosa in a tense still voice.

'It's such weather!' said auntie cheerfully, and went into the pantry to take off her shoes. The shoes fell on the floor with a dull sound; she knew it was not the weather that kept Stephen away; he did not want to come. All the glory of her thank-offering had faded; now she would have to ask father for money for the bazaar.

Robert had come to see Blanche; when the rain began he

carried her back from the veranda to her bed, near the tablet, so that she could put out her hand and stroke Echo's ear. She had grown so much while she was in bed that her mauve cotton frock barely reached to her knees. When Robert took her up in his arms she had to hold it down for decency.

'Oh, I wish I could have some new dress,' she moaned.

'If I had any money,' said Robert, 'I should take you, Blanche, and we should buy the best silk in the market and the tailor should make you a dress.'

'Oh, I wish you had some money, Bob.'

It was at that moment that auntie came in and asked: 'Have you any money, Bob?'

Robert flushed, for auntie knew he had none; if she had not been so distracted she could not have asked him that.

'Have I ever any money?' he said bitterly.

Auntie was distracted. In the early morning she would have to go to the bazaar to buy the daily food; Joseph and the children must be fed and she had spent the money. St Rock, St Thomas More, the Little Rose of China, of what avail were they to her now? She went into the pantry, her lips moving in prayer, but she found herself repeating, 'Smoked hilsa, curry, carrot juice,' as if they were the names of saints.

'If only I had some money,' cried Robert, and auntie was thinking the same. Long, long ago her money had gone; Adolf Kempf had taken most of it. Indeed he would not have gone so soon had he known there was any left; and the rest she had given, a little here, a little there: for the children's clothes, to help Joseph out of a difficulty, to pay for a pair of shoes to be mended or for Belle's tooth to be drilled, until it was gone. If it had not been that her sister, the children's mother, had had the sense to leave her money in trust for them so that father could not draw it out, they would have been penniless. Father did not remember that auntie had given her money, she herself could not have told where it had gone, but now she wished that she could have kept back a little just to pay for her offering, the first money she had spent for herself in years, and then she would not have had to ask father for that five rupees.

'Joseph, can I have a little money for the bazaar?'

Father wanted to know what she had done with the five rupees he gave her yesterday. Where were they? Where were those five rupees?

'Blanche's medicines,' auntie pleaded.

'And the medicine bill had just now come! You're lying to me, Anna. What have you done with the money?'

'I – I lost it.'

'*Lost* it! Lost five whole rupees. How could you lose it?' Father was appalled.

Auntie thought of a story about a pickpocket in the tram, a dozen stories came into her head, but she could not tell any of them. Already the virtue had gone out of her thank-offering by reason of her lies. In one desperate rush she told father the truth and waited for the storm to burst above her head.

'Only a little money, Joseph, and I shall manage. Only give me a little—'

'I haven't any money!' shouted father. 'I tell you I haven't—'

He remembered. Slowly from his pocket he drew a cheque, creased and dirty: 'Pay cash, one hundred rupees.'

# 20

It was September, and the rains were drawing to a close; there was a week of hot sunny weather before the next day's rain, and the heat was intense. The last weeks of heat before the cold weather were the worst to bear; people who had gone cheerfully through May and June and the dragging months of rain flagged now in September; it seemed impossible to live through the heat until the poojah festivals set them free for a holiday in October, free to go on leave to the hills, to camp, to the sea.

Mr deSouza's house was quiet; the Bartons' and the Mascareneses' suites were closed, Mr Kawashima was ill.

The house had suffered badly in the rains, the walls were mottled with damp, mildew, and a fungus that spread in green and greasy patches, the wood of the shutters had swelled and they would not close properly; the garden looked derelict, leaves and earth swept up in ridges on the lawn, the water lying stagnant in the drains. Already it had a graveyard smell, and still Mr deSouza was mysterious and obstinate and would not do the repairs.

'The house looks as if it will fall,' Robert warned him. 'You'll never let these empty suites with the place in such a state. Do you want to ruin it?'

'What I want is my business, and you can tell your friends, those Lemarchants, that if they do not pay their rent I shall turn them out. Yes, tell them that,' said Mr deSouza to Robert, and laughed.

'Why do you laugh?' cried Robert. 'Do you think that's funny?'

'I do,' chuckled Mr deSouza, 'and I'll tell you for why, Bob. It will frighten them into paying for fear they must shift, but they will have to go all the same.'

'What do you mean?' asked Robert, but Mr deSouza would not explain.

Father had meant to pay the rent from the one hundred rupees, but he had not been able to resist the money in his pocket; he gave auntie twenty rupees, and she, unable to resist it either, bought a coat for Blanche of plum-coloured flannel with a strange collar called 'hare', that Blanche thought meant 'hair'.

'A coat *now* when it is so hot!' she said.

'But you must have a coat.'

'Why must I when I needed a dress?' said Blanche, but she loved the coat all the same, and thought how, when it was cold, she would walk past the Fernandeses in it on her way to school.

Father had bought a Tundice that at present would not work, it had taken most of his money. The rent could not be paid, but Robert advised them not to worry. 'I wouldn't pay it. My father has some plan; he wouldn't tell me, but I think he will make you shift.'

'Shift from *here*!' said Rosa indignantly. 'Oh, we couldn't. You couldn't make us. Not now. *We* discovered the tablet, Robert. This house belonged to our relations. In a way it is our place.'

'You have no right to it,' said Robert; 'he can turn you out if he wishes. Not a stone of it is yours.'

'It *ought* to be ours, besides we've been here all these years. Why does he want us to go?'

'You haven't paid your rent,' Robert reminded her gently, 'but I think he has some other reason. Something he is going to do with the house.'

'He *can't* do anything to this part of it without our permission,' said Rosa grandly. 'The tablet was put up to our relation.'

'You can't prove even that,' said Robert.

'You don't want us to. You're jealous. He can't do anything to this suite. It is consecrated.'

'That is what I say,' said auntie. 'And we should not go on living in it, having tea and tiffin and what all in a consecrated place. It makes me very uncomfortable. I shall be glad to go.'

'I won't go,' said Rosa.

'Nor shall I,' cried Blanche, but auntie was pleased at the idea. 'He will turn us out,' she said hopefully, 'and in that case he could hardly expect us to pay our rent, could he?'

'I shall say I will not go,' said Blanche.

'Then they will take you – like this,' and Robert picked her up and put her out of the door. Blanche gave a scream of fury, her face turned crimson, she fell on Robert with her fists, beating and thumping him, and then wept with despair. They could not comfort her. When Robert swept her up she had felt for a moment the horror of a force that could not be broken, her helplessness to stand against it, to prevent it, her insignificance; and that night she woke crying that she had lost Echo, and though he was there on the wall she still cried that he was lost. Rosa stayed by her until she fell asleep again; little Blanche who had set her heart on what she could not have.

Rosa could see how useless it was for Blanche to set her heart on Echo, she could pity her because she knew that she could never have him, 'and yet,' she whispered hopelessly to herself, 'I can't help myself for setting my heart on Stephen.' Already she was learning to do without him, to live all day, to lie at night, alone, and that filled her with despair. It was the beginning of the end.

For eleven days he had not come, eleven days that had been cruel to her. From the beginning she had known that if she let Stephen touch her the enchantment would be spoiled, from that night when she had so wanted him to kiss her that she could hold out against him no longer, it was gone. It seemed to her now that the blood of Rosabelle and Claude had little to do with her, hers was the easy sensuous oriental-tinged blood of her mother's family. Even Belle was colder than she. That made her cry out all the more for Stephen, for something her blood had known, sweet and satisfying, and to Stephen it had meant no more than the moment, he could go away leaving her for ever hungry. She began to think that auntie was right, and that it would be good for them to leave the house, for now the words of Rosabelle's inscription and her unicorn were mocking her, the LeViste banner flaunting close on the unicorn's shoulder.

Stephen had a letter from his mother, one of her affectionate, tactful letters that he knew so well:

D. has been asked by Uncle George to come out for the cold weather, sailing on the *Mooltan* October 17th, and Catherine Scott is going with her.

('Ha!' cried his father, shying off at once.)

They will be in Calcutta for the polo, so nice if they could stay on and be with you for a while, perhaps you could arrange it. P.G.'s, of course. Am writing to Sir Thomas. So nice for you and D. to be together.

I can imagine it, thought Stephen. A letter from Tommy or William – God! if it's William I'll have his skin; and mother reading it aloud at breakfast: 'Stephen mixed up with some little Anglo-Indian girl! Stephen! What can we do? It's unthinkable, my Stephen! I told you he shouldn't go out there. Something must be done.'

And father: 'Leave the boy alone. He'll come round. I don't suppose he's serious.'

'Sir Thomas, or William, wouldn't have written if it was *not* serious. That's just like you, Henry. Never do anything until it's too late. I shall talk it over with nannie. She's always so sensible.'

Upstairs in the nursery: 'Nannie, it's Stephen. We're rather worried.'

'Stephen?' Nannie in her comfortable slow voice. 'What has he been doing now?'

'There's Uncle George in Delhi.' That would be nannie, by and by. 'Why not send D. out to him, then she could see Stephen.'

To Nannie, Delhi and Calcutta were like London and Brighton, an hour in the train; just as she always imagined Stephen walking in a topee through a jungle full of blazing sun, palm trees, snakes and tigers.

'She could take a friend to travel with.' And in both their minds they went through the catalogue of Stephen's girl friends.

They had been clever over Catherine Scott. Stephen had to

admit that. She was not the most obvious of his girl friends, and Stephen had not thought that anyone noticed how much he had cared for her. Catherine had turned up her nose at him, but if she was willing to come out with D. ... Stephen drew circles on his blotting paper, remembering her. She came to Totnes for the holidays as a tall schoolgirl with an ash-gold plait, and Stephen had met her afterwards in London, still tall, still palely gold; pretty and witty and nice to handle, with clothes that did not leap to the eye but lingered there. He read the letter again and scowled. Mother had been a little too clever; 'so nice for you and D. to be together', when she meant quite plainly 'so nice if you will like being with Catherine and she succeeds in detaching you from that miserable girl'. He was suddenly hot with anger for Rosa, Rosa against them all; Tommy and William, mother, Catherine, nannie, D., against Rosa, against him; sailing in to save him, not trusting him to manage his own affairs, treating him like a silly child.

'I'm going to marry Rosa,' he told William that night.

'Are you? On what?' asked William amicably.

'On what? I don't understand.'

'Well, you'll be sacked. Of course your people may give you an allowance, but should you think that likely?'

'I can get another job.'

'Don't be childish, Stephen. Where do you think you'd get another job on pay as good as you're getting now? Even if you weren't sacked you couldn't live on your pay.'

'I think I ought to marry her,' said Stephen.

'Do you mean she's going to have a baby?'

'Good God, no!' shouted Stephen. 'I mean I – well, you wouldn't understand, but I think I should marry her.'

'There is only one thing that could justify your marrying her,' said William seriously, 'and that is if you really loved her, and then you'd have to love her a hell of a lot. It's hard enough for two people to go on loving one another in an ordinary marriage, and this would be far harder. Have you really thought about it? You would probably have to resign from the Saturday Club. If you come up for election at Tolly you'd be black-balled.'

'Much I'd care.'

'You would care later on. You can sneer at Clubs, but they're very pleasant places to belong to. It's hard to live in a community and not do as they do.'

'They're sheep,' said Stephen furiously, 'just sheep.'

'But quite nice sheep,' suggested William.

'Too bloody nice. God help you if you're the least bit different.'

'Now I wonder,' said William, 'what makes you so sure you're not a sheep, Stephen. I think you'll soon find that you are if you marry Rosa, that you'll long to be back in the herd where you belong. You see, I fail to see anything outstanding about you, and you would have to be very outstanding to do a thing like this and make a success of it. It's one of those things in life that are too easy to do and too hard to make a success of, too hard for someone with a character like yours.'

'Thanks,' said Stephen; 'but anyhow I'd take her home.'

'She'd be out of it there too, with your friends and your family.'

'They'd be nice to her for my sake.'

'That would be nice for her!'

'At home it would be no more than if I'd married a foreigner.'

'What about your children?' asked William. 'How would you feel if one of them were dark?'

'Rosa's perfectly fair.'

'Her little sister's dark, you said so.'

Stephen was silent and William said gently: 'And you don't really love her, you know you don't Stephen, though she may love you, poor girl.'

'Then isn't it mean not to marry her?'

'Oh, don't talk like a schoolboy. Wouldn't it be far *meaner*, as you call it, to marry her and not to love her. A nice time you'd give her. God's patience, Stephen, you know quite well you only want to marry her because you think we're trying to stop you.'

'And aren't you?'

'Yes, and it's extraordinarily decent of us. Now shut up and go away. I want to read.'

Stephen went into his room and sat on his bed, and immediately all the eyes in his photographs seemed to fix themselves on him: mother, father, Janet, D., nannie, even Catherine, though she was looking down at her glove.

There was not one particle of Rosa in his room, he had nothing of her at all, she alone had never tried to impress herself on him. How slight, how fragile a hold she had taken, the least movement and he could shake her off. It was as if, compared to human hands, fairy fingers had touched him and like a fairy touch it haunted him, it had gone through his flesh to his bones. Among the Williams, the Catherines, the other people, she was romance; the faint elusive romance of her home that was in the house with Rosabelle's tablet, the garden with her sundial, the shield, and the fabulous unicorn, the weeping trees in the cemetery; and it seemed to him that if he let her go this would be the end of it; of his youth, of romance, of that first hot fire of delight, of the radiance he had known, and he could not bear to let it go.

He wrote to her that night:

I have something to tell you, Rosa. I love you and I want you to marry me. I am coming myself to tell you. Be ready for me after five. There's a kiss in this letter.

STEPHEN

The peon who took Stephen's letter put his pass-book on his desk.

# 21

Auntie, in the middle of her cooking, took the letter from the peon, and holding it between her finger and thumb to stain it as little as she could, carried it in to Rosa.

Rosa was typing at the dressing-table with the typewriter kept steady by the handle of a brush, and as she took each sheet off the roller she sat with it in her hand, staring out at the garden or up at the tablet until father from the next room cried: 'Rosa, get on.' She was dressed in a limp blue cotton, her face was sticky with heat, and she had tied her hair back with her belt. When auntie gave her the letter a dark blush stole up her neck to her face, and drops of sweat broke out on her upper lip and forehead. She read the words as if she did not believe them and began to tremble.

'What is it?' said auntie in a whisper. 'Is it bad? You look so frightened.'

Rosa put out her hand and clutched her. 'It's Stephen. Oh, auntie!'

'What has he said to you now?' whispered auntie fiercely. 'Oh, I should like to see him to tell him what I think of him. Mr

Harman was a bad man, but see what he did for Belle, and what good has Stephen ever done for you, Rosa? What good?'

'Hush,' said Rosa, drawing auntie nearer and leaning her head on her shoulder. 'Hush, auntie. Listen, for this will make you happy. Stephen is coming this afternoon, and, auntie, he has asked me to marry him.'

Auntie simply could not believe it. She had seen the letter, she had made the arrangements, but still she could not believe it. It was impossible. Even when she had sent for the tailor to come at once with Rosa's yellow organza, even when the yellow organza came floating down the street and Rosa had it on with her pearl ear-rings and had looked in the mirror a hundred times, asking auntie if her hair were all right, still she knew it was impossible.

There was no one in the house but Rosa and auntie. Auntie would not leave Rosa alone with Stephen now that she was to be engaged, she had her principles, and especially was it not right when you remembered that the suite was a chapel. 'I will stay in the bedroom,' she told Rosa, 'but it wouldn't do for me to be out altogether.'

The thought of marriage had at once made auntie coy and careful. Rosa smiled when she thought how easily and carelessly auntie had let her and Belle slip through her fingers. She smiled regretfully; in the bedroom she had a chaperon and a unicorn. She wished they could really be hers, hers, and not a sham.

Blanche had been sent to sit on the deSouzas' veranda, for Mr deSouza was out and Mrs deSouza was kind. She gave Blanche a fan and a glass of fizzy lemonade and Robert came out and sat with her.

'What's happening, Blanche?'

'They wouldn't tell me, but I think it's Stephen coming to

marry Rosa. She has been to have her hair set and auntie spent the bazaar money for flowers.'

'Oh,' said Robert, and sat looking at the veranda rails. Presently Blanche saw that he was crying.

'Do you mind so much?' she cried. 'Oh, Bob, please, please don't cry. I'll marry you, Bob, as soon as I'm fourteen. Mrs Anthony says I shall be old enough then. Please don't cry, Bob.'

Father went when he was asked to go out, with none of the shouting and roaring he usually made.

'Stephen is coming,' said auntie, and he went without a word. Afterwards she remembered that she had thought it peculiar at the time.

At five o'clock they were ready, Rosa in the sitting-room, auntie in the bedroom; at six o'clock when the light in the room was dim and uncertain so that Rosa's yellow dress had changed to a wine gold, and the garden was golden too, as the sun sank down and the fly-catcher birds were rising on whirring wings, they were waiting still.

Rosa moved about the room, fidgeting with her dress, looking in the mirror, polishing her nails, fanning herself with her handkerchief, but auntie sat still by her bed in a dream; only her ears were awake, listening for Stephen, and she did not believe he would come.

The light faded as the minutes went by; now the corners were in dusk, the head of each bed in shadow, the pillows shone. Now there was only a ladder of light up the wall, it came to rest on the unicorn and struck sparks of gold from his hooves and touched his horn with creamy light.

Auntie stiffened in her chair, for someone was coming, not Stephen, but someone with loose shoes that clipper-cloppered up and down. She heard a knock and going fearfully to peep through the curtain, she saw a peon from Stephen's office, a chit-book in his hand and his umbrella hooked into the back of his collar.

'Auntee! Come here!' Rosa's voice was sharp with fear. 'Auntie, why has he sent me a note? Why hasn't he come?'

'It is to say he has been kept, that is all,' auntie soothed her. 'You must sign here.'

Rosa signed, trembling, in the book: 'Rosa Lemarchant,' in her spiky tremulous writing.

'Take it. I can't open it,' said Rosa, and auntie unwillingly took the note, but her fingers shook so that she could hardly open the envelope.

'What does it say? Why hasn't he come?' Rosa's cheeks were white under her rouge. 'Tell me, auntie. Tell me.'

'I don't know what he means,' said auntie in a bewildered whisper. 'When have you hidden a cheque? When—'

'Give it to me,' Rosa snatched the letter away. 'Auntee!' she cried, catching her breath, 'Oh, auntee,' and began to whimper, 'I don't know what he means. What is he talking about? What have I done?'

Stephen had written the letter when he was angry, and his anger burned in the sentences, burned them into Rosa's brain as she tried to read the letter.

You cheated me. You pretended not to take it. You thought I would forget ... stealing ... pass-book. If I hadn't found out in time ... I never want to see you again.

STEPHEN

Out of a long-distance Rosa saw auntie's face, where a tear

was caught in a wrinkle. She put out a hand to touch it. Why was auntie weeping? For her? For Stephen?

Someone was telling her to sit down, was taking her by the arm to force her into a chair. Her face was down on the table-cloth, a smell of dust in her nostrils, and she heard auntie call 'Boy! Boy! bring a glass of water. Quickly, Boy.' The tumbler was against her teeth, the ice rattled, she could hardly sip it. Auntie took her handkerchief and wrung it out in the water and dabbed it on Rosa's forehead.

'Did I faint?' asked Rosa. She heard the flycatchers' cry as they rose up in the garden and saw that the sun had gone down. 'It's dark,' she said in a whisper.

'Drink your water,' said auntie.

'N-not after you've put your hanky in it,' said Rosa in peals of laughter; she laughed, rocking herself backwards and for-wards, laughing higher and higher until she caught sight of herself in the mirror and her laughter ceased abruptly. She looked at herself, pressing her fingers against her mouth to stop it shaking. How ghastly she looked in that yellow dress, the smears of rouge on her cheeks, her hair fallen sideways, her working mouth. As she had begun to laugh, now she began to cry, more and more loudly, until she hardly knew what she was crying for.

Had she swallowed the ice? Her stomach was rising. It was not the ice, something hot and sour-tasting rose in her mouth.

'*Auntee!*' she screamed, 'I'm going to be sick.'

'Run, run,' cried auntie. 'Oh, *not* on the carpet, Rosa.'

## 22

Auntie burned a feather under Rosa's nose and the filthy smell of its burning made her cough and sneeze. 'Oh, take it away,' she cried, 'or I shall be sick again.'

Auntie threw it out of the window and came and sat down by the bed. She put her hands on her knees as she sat and looked solemnly at Rosa.

'What is it?' asked Rosa fretfully. 'I can't talk to you just now, auntie. Leave me alone for a little while, please.'

That was all she wanted now, to be left alone, to lie in darkness and hide her face. She was too hurt to talk or cry. Oh, why could auntie not go away and leave her alone?

'Rosa,' said auntie very solemnly, 'have you been sick before like this?'

'No, why?' said Rosa. 'Must you ask me this now?'

'You are sure you haven't been sick?'

'Of course I'm sure.'

'Have you thought why you were sick? What made you faint again so that Boy and I had to carry you to bed? Have you thought of that?'

'It was enough to make me sick and faint. It was the shock,' said Rosa defensively.

'I have seen people faint for grief and shock,' said auntie, 'but I have never seen them vomit, at least not immediately.'

'I did,' said Rosa, but her heart began to beat loudly.

'Not from grief,' auntie said again, 'not from grief. I think you are going to have a baby, Rosa.'

'No,' said Rosa quickly and licked her lips. 'No, I'm not, auntie.' Auntie sat there like an old toad by her bed, catching her silly flies of answers. 'It isn't possible. I tell you, Stephen has taken care. You wouldn't understand, but nowadays people wear things so there isn't any fear.'

Auntie took no notice. 'Have you had your menses this month?'

'N-no, but that is nothing. I'm often irregular.'

'Did you have it last month?'

'Oh, *auntee*! Leave me alone.'

'God help us,' said auntie. 'And we have quarrelled with Mrs Anthony.'

The sounds of the street came in through the window, for an Indian city is never quiet. There are the crows and the myriad insects and where Indians are together there is chatter; now the commotion of the street came into the room where Rosa lay on her bed and auntie sat, staring into the corner.

'There is bad luck for us all,' she said at last.

'Stephen brought us bad luck; he broke the jasmine when I told him not to.'

'He has broken worse than jasmine,' said auntie bitterly; 'and now what is to be done?'

'We must tell the doctor and he will take it away.'

'I hate to tell that doctor anything, and it is murder, Rosa!'

She sat running it over in her mind, confused. 'Supposing,' she hesitated, 'supposing we gave it out that Mr Kempf had come back, and I would go away to be with him and take you with me. After being with Mr Kempf, who, after all, is my husband, you understand, Rosa, would it be surprising if I were to have a baby?'

Rosa thought that that might be a little too surprising; delicately she said: 'But you are rather old, auntie.'

Already auntie saw herself with a dear baby and was planning to bring it up as she had brought up the others. She would wrap it in layers of wool and give it too much to eat, spoil it and slap it by turns, and have it baptized Joseph Gervase Stephen, because it would be a boy.

'He could pass as mine,' she said with satisfaction. 'That's a good plan. I will have the baby, Rosa.'

Rosa moved fretfully on her pillow and thought how ridiculous auntie was.

'And where do you think we could go where we're not known?'

'Somewhere a great way off. Poona.'

'Why Poona?'

'I have always thought that Poona sounded a nice place, Rosa.'

Rosa laughed hopelessly. 'Who is to pay for us to go there? How should we live when we have gone?'

'Belle,' hazarded auntie.

'*She* wouldn't. Besides, she may have gone to England herself.'

'Rosa, it's Stephen who should help us. Stephen should provide for his child.'

'Stephen! If you tell one word of this to Stephen I shall *kill* myself. You hear me, auntie, I mean it. You must promise me.

Promise me you won't speak to anyone. I shall manage it myself. Promise, auntie. Haven't I shame enough, already?'

'It's your father who is to blame,' said auntie, with sudden conviction, when she had soothed her. 'For where else did he get the money? It was your father who took the cheque. I'm sure of it.'

'Then he must go to Stephen and tell him. He must tell him that I didn't do it,' cried Rosa wildly.

'That would be bad, to let your father take the blame.'

'Why should I suffer for a cheat? Why should I be called a cheat for him?'

'Children have to suffer for their fathers, Rosa,' said auntie. 'You know we are taught that from the beginning.'

'It doesn't matter,' she said, sinking down on the pillow; 'it wasn't only the cheque, I see that now. It wasn't only the cheque, or father, or all of you. I made it impossible myself, all the time.'

Auntie was silent. She was remembering the money she had taken from Stephen for the bazaar.

'I didn't take it; I borrowed it,' thought auntie, and at once it were as if a voice asked her: 'Did you pay it back?'

'What do you think?' she asked Blanche that evening; 'should I tell Rosa that I took money from Stephen?'

Blanche's ill little face was haggard with sympathy; she was so tired that her legs were staggering, but she listened carefully to auntie and she said, 'Perhaps you need not tell her, auntie, because Stephen was your friend, too. If he lent you the money it was apart from Rosa. It was your fault, not hers. It will do no good to tell her. But now I *hate* father.'

She took her new coat that she loved from the cupboard, and hurled it down on the floor at father's feet.

'Here, what's this?' said father. 'What are you doing with the new coat I bought you?'

'You didn't buy it, Stephen did,' said Blanche stormily. 'You stole the money, it was Stephen's money and now because of you he won't marry Rosa.' And backing to the door, out of his reach, she shouted: 'Robber. Liar. Thief!' and darted out before he could catch her.

'What she says is true,' cried auntie. 'What trouble you have put us all in, Joseph. Didn't you find a cheque that Stephen tried to give Rosa and she refused? Didn't you take it to the bank and get the money for it? Didn't you, Joseph?'

'No. I did not. Would I, Anna, do a thing like that, I ask you?'

'If you ask me, you would,' said auntie. 'Where else did you get the money?'

'It was the races—'

'Joseph, you're lying. You took Stephen's cheque and it was that money you spent on your Tundice, which is a loss, and on this coat.' Auntie picked it up and brushed the collar. 'This coat,' she repeated, 'that now we have got, we may as well take care of. Then Stephen wrote that he wanted to marry Rosa.' And forgetting that father was the villain she told him the whole story.

'You say he *wrote* in a letter that he wanted her to marry him?' asked father thoughtfully.

'He did indeed.'

'Has she kept that letter?'

'Has she ever parted with it? All his notes, every little thing she keeps.'

'Tell her to bring them to me.'

'Father is very angry with Stephen,' said auntie, going in to Rosa where she was lying on the bed.

'*Father* is angry?' said Rosa. 'That's funny!'

'He wants to see the letters, Rosa. Let me show them to him.'

'Show him my letters! Show them to that lying old thief!'

'He is your father, Rosa,' said auntie patiently. 'I think you should show him your letters when he tells you. None of you children treat your father properly.'

'After all he has done, you can still say that? Really, auntie, you behave as if you were his dog.'

'No, I do not,' said auntie indignantly; 'just now I was rude to him myself, but I am his wife's sister, not his daughter.'

'Rosa,' called father over the partition, for he had heard every word they had said, 'Rosa, I'm so sorry and unhappy for what I have done. Rosa, let your father see if he can help you. Let him at least try to undo the harm he has done. Where are the letters?'

'I can't show them.'

'Rosa,' cried father, coming into the bedroom and kneeling down by her bed. Taking her hand, he began to talk to her, soothing and coaxing, pleading with her. 'Don't refuse this to me, don't turn me away. You mustn't, you can't. Please Rosa, don't let me go all my life with this sin on my soul. Rosa, forgive me, show me the letters.'

'You can't refuse him,' said auntie, much moved. 'Oh Rosa, you can't refuse him.'

Reluctantly, suspiciously, Rosa drew the letters out from under her pillow, and gave them to him.

'My little child,' said father fondly, opening Stephen's first letter, 'my loving little child. H'm!' he said as he read the few lines, 'Good! We can run him in for breach of promise.'

Rosa started up. '*What* did you say?' But father carried the letters into the sitting-room. She ran after him in her bare feet, the yellow dress creased and tumbled with lying on the bed, her face streaked with sweat and tears. 'Give me my letters, father. What do you mean to do?'

'Tell me,' said father, turning round and taking her by the chin. 'Don't lie to me or I'll beat you, big girl as you are. You lived with Stephen Bright, didn't you?'

'Yes,' breathed Rosa.

'Good!' said father. 'And he said if you did he would marry you. That was what he said, didn't he?'

'No! No! No!' lied Rosa passionately. 'We never thought of anything like that. We never thought of marrying.'

'Listen, Rosa,' said father, his face close to hers, 'you will say that he did promise to marry you. You will say that. Do you hear?'

Rosa's eyes, looking into his, were like a frightened animal's; she was losing control of herself. 'Give me my letters,' she screamed. 'Oh! help me auntie. Blanche, help me. Make him give me my letters.'

Blanche darted forward and snatched them from father's hand. 'Don't let him take them, Blanche,' cried Rosa, 'burn them quickly. Put them in the fire.'

Blanche, shaking all over, ran into the pantry where Boy had dinner cooking on the stove, she pushed the pan away and threw the letters in the fire; the pan went over with all the meat and vegetables, the flames sprang up on the paper, there was a smell of burning fat.

'*Ari-bap!*' cried Boy, flapping with his duster.

'Oh! Oh! Oh!' screamed auntie; for this was worse to her than any breach of promise.

Blanche gave one panic-stricken look at father and ran out the back way. She had not run for weeks, her heart pounded so that she almost choked on every step; she dragged herself up the stairs to the deSouzas' flat to find Robert, and there on the dark veranda in Robert's arms, she sobbed out all the story.

'And I daren't go back, for this time father will beat me. And we shall have nothing to eat because I burned it all, and auntie is so angry, but I didn't mean to, Robert. I didn't mean to, but he was hurting Rosa. I had to leave her, and by now he may have *killed* her,' said Blanche luridly; and though neither she nor Robert were very brave, they went downstairs together.

But father had done nothing. He had simply looked at the burning letters as if he, too, were going to cry. 'I might have got you five thousand rupees,' he said piteously. 'Never have we had a chance before like this, and you girls have ruined it all. You will take no notice of me, and now you have lost us five thousand rupees. No notice. You never have. Now see what you have lost.'

'There now!' said auntie. 'Haven't I always told you that? You don't treat your father properly.'

'We couldn't do a thing like that,' called Rosa from the bedroom, where she had fled. 'There are some things we can't do even for money.'

Belle had said: 'We all will do anything for money,' but that was long ago. Now they knew that the blood of the LeVistes ran in their veins and that the Lemarchants went back to the days of the East India Company; they were an old, proud family. She cried that out to father, flinging the words at him in her shrillest voice. And suddenly her protests died.

She was standing before the tablet. The serene tempered words seemed as far removed from hers, screamed in defiance of father, as she herself was from the Lady Rosabelle.

Consecrated to the memory of Rosabelle (née LeViste) for one day the wife of Joseph Paul Lemarchant, who died on the evening of her wedding day, 12th October 1792, aged seventeen years and is buried innocent and virgin, in this foreign land.

Erected by her husband in grief too deep to express in the Name of her blessed Redeemer and hope of forgiveness.

Aloof and delicate, they disdained the room and Rosa, even Echo had turned his back, and the little unicorn, for ever pacing with his banner, the signet of Rosabelle, was not for her. She was still the same Rosa Lemarchant who was no one, who told lies, the child of insignificance, without hope or help, whom Stephen could not love without disgrace.

'Damn the unicorn!' cried Rosa in a storm of fury. She let her voice rise even more shrilly, and her hands gesticulated. 'I can't stand them any longer. I can't bear them. Damn her and the unicorn.' She lifted up the door brick and hurled it at the tablet.

It hit it with a crash, but the marble did not break; not a splinter showed, but at the corner of the unicorn's mouth was a crack, a thread in the stone, and now the unicorn had a smile.

# 23

'You mean,' said Robert, 'that if you hadn't thought that your family was descended from that Joseph Lemarchant and the LeVistes, if you hadn't found the tablets and seen the Lady here and in the cemetery, you would have done this to Stephen?'

'Why do you care?' asked Rosa.

'I care in two ways,' said Robert slowly. 'For one thing I think it's only the people with silly minds who care more who they are than what they are.'

'You think I have a silly mind,' said Rosa quietly, where before she would have flared up at Robert if he had dared to say that.

'You have, you know,' said Robert. 'You thought I was jealous because I didn't like your talk of families and ancestors and tradition; it wasn't the talk I hated but the idea, the idea so many of our people have had, that to be ourselves is a disgrace. You said: "I am one of an old, great European family, therefore I am too proud to run this Stephen Bright in for breach of promise and have it brought out in court that he would not marry me." I think you would have been prouder if you could have said, "I am Rosa Lemarchant; not for all the money in the world would *I* do such a thing."'

'Do you feel like that, Robert?' Rosa looked up at him, for she was sitting on the steps while he stood against a pillar; the porch was dark, she could see only the glimmer of his white shirt and the shadow of his face beside the pillar. 'Do you feel like that? I believe you do. That's why they always respect you. In you there's something that can't be touched, but I – oh! Robert, you don't know what I have been like.'

Sometimes it was trouble, full of pain and thoughts of Stephen; in the night it was a crying need for Stephen, an agony of regret and blame; for hours it was like the dull sky above a river, that sees neither cloud nor colour, but the blank reflection of itself. Sometimes to ease the pain she pretended, making a castle that tumbled to pieces at a breath, and there was always fear and worry, nagging at her like auntie.

'But how – how?'

'I can go to that doctor and he'll take it away.'

'That's murder. You would kill your child,' said auntie.

'Better for it to be killed than to live,' said Rosa drearily. 'No one thinks like that now.'

'I do,' said auntie. 'I think it's wicked to destroy your child, Rosa.'

'Oh, *you*,' said Rosa. 'Don't call it my child, auntie. It is only the size of a thimble now, if it is a child at all.'

In spite of that she did not want the doctor to take it away. She had a sudden vision of herself carrying Stephen's son through the garden; she saw a baby with yellow hair and a scowl, as she carried him through the garden she felt his hands on her neck and, presently, she picked a snapdragon flower and fitted it on his finger. 'Now the dragon has bitten you,' she said.

It was so clear that she was sure that it was true, and the baby was not the sort of baby that she would have imagined, not happy and laughing, but grave, with a little tallow face and yellow hair. Now, instead of wondering how to be rid of it, she was plotting to keep it.

She sat in the porch with Robert; though she would not walk with him in the garden, she often sat with him there on the steps. Indeed she seemed to be seeking him out; though he was still sore and stinging from the hurt she had given him, he was gentle and friendly with her, but he did not flatter her now, he told her the truth. That September night there were no fireflies, no jasmine scent; there was a new moon threaded on a circle of gold, a new hope, that early dropped behind the palms. A wind came from the garden and puffed around their feet, blowing the folds of Rosa's skirts, and it too dropped away, knowing it could not thrill them now, leaving the porch quiet and still.

'Did Stephen see the Lady?' asked Robert suddenly.

'No. For two or three nights or more, he waited for her and saw nothing. Wasn't it strange, Robert, that Stephen began it, opened our eyes for us, and yet he could see nothing himself?'

'Perhaps he didn't feel enough,' said Robert. 'He didn't begin it for me. I saw her before he came, and yet – I was jealous of him even when I didn't know that it was Stephen I was jealous of, so perhaps in a way he did. Think of the times we have seen it, only when our feelings were roused very much, when they were deep and intense and not for ourselves, feelings for some-one else. With me it was jealousy; and Mr Mascarenes thought his baby was dead, and auntie had been tired and worried.'

'And I had found that Belle had gone again with Mr Harman, and I had found the sundial with Stephen.' Rosa was silent in the pain of remembering that night.

'Blanche wanted a dog so badly. Perhaps that was why she saw Echo continually, and only Echo.'

'That wasn't a deep feeling.'

'How do you know? That may have to be the most intense feeling any of us have had. I'm sure we can only see when our feeling is very deep, and I think that is the same the other way on. Have you ever thought, Rosa, why it is that only a few of the people who have died come back to us as ghosts?'

'Stephen said they're not ghosts, that all our lives are going on at the same moment; that past and present and future are all one, but that must be nonsense Robert.'

'No, not nonsense,' said Robert. 'Death is a thing we can't understand, nor what is after death, nor before life. The church tells us but they can't know. Perhaps because there is no death, no time, the people we see as ghosts are only the people who for a moment have broken through to our lives.'

'Yet we always see them doing the same thing,' objected Rosa; 'time after time the same thing. We always see the Lady crying and running into the chapel.'

'If all her life were photographed, those moments which she felt most would come out most clearly, be the easiest for *us* to see. When her father left her, she felt it intensely, we know she did; perhaps of her life that moment was the most intense in feeling and we, taken out of ourselves with grief or jealousy or shock and strain, could see her where normally we might have missed her. I think if we forgot ourselves, turned ourselves in, we might see a great deal more.'

'If she killed herself, and I think she did kill herself, why didn't we see that, Robert? That must have been more intense even.'

'She may not have killed herself here, it wouldn't be easy

unless she threw herself over the stairs. I think she must have done it outside the house or it would be here. We have only seen her run into the chapel.'

'And Stephen never saw her,' sighed Rosa.

'Stephen was a selfish person, his feelings were always for himself,' said Robert quickly, 'even with you. I don't think he loved you very much, Rosa.'

Rosa stood up beside Robert on the steps and laid her hand on his arm. 'Do you?' she asked. 'Do you love me very much, Robert?'

'You know I do.'

'Enough to do what I ask you?'

'Ask me anything.'

'Will you marry me, Robert?'

'Of course I will,' said Robert doubtfully, with the thought of his father at the back of his mind.

'Now?'

'Now? Why now? Why not wait till I get work?'

'I'm going to have a baby,' said Rosa.

He nodded. 'I thought you were, but you can't do that, you know.'

'I must, and I want you to help me, Bob.'

'But Rosa,' he took her by her elbows which were cold in his hands. 'Rosa,' he shook her gently, for she seemed not to hear him, to notice him. 'I can't let you have a baby. Stephen's baby. I should hate it.'

'You wouldn't. You think you would but you wouldn't when it was there. You'd like it. You like babies. Remember how you helped with the Mascareneses' baby.'

'That's different, and what would we do with it? You don't know anything about them; besides, they're very expensive.

Don't you understand, it will be difficult enough without that. We haven't any money Rosa, we can't get any, just our bare living if we're lucky, something more if we're tremendously lucky. Alone we have a chance to succeed; it will be difficult but there is still a chance. If we burden ourselves with this baby there'll be no chance at all.'

'I want it,' said Rosa obstinately.

'You can't have it. You must see the doctor and make him take it away.'

'No!' Rosa burst into tears. 'No! Bob, don't make me do that. You're the only one who has ever helped us and understood us. Let me have my baby, Bob. Please, please help me.' She pushed him back and looked at him with tear-wet eyes, clinging to him. 'It is wrong to say this to you, but I was so proud to be with Stephen, I loved him. Oh Bob, help me to keep a little bit of him.'

Robert began to laugh, he leaned against the pillar and laughed into the darkness. 'Help you to keep a little of him. Rosa, that's too funny! Help you to keep a little bit of Stephen! Exactly what you are asking me to do!'

He pushed her away and clenched his fists, for a moment she thought that he would hit her. 'Can't you forget him?' he cried.

The wind came again and rustled the palm-leaves. The moon had gone, the garden was hidden and dark and the rustling trees sounded like thin paper.

'Oh, I can't! I can't!' Rosa buried her face in her hands and wept.

# 24

Mr deSouza had sold the house to a syndicate of which he was to be one of the directors; it was to be pulled down and the site used for the building of a mammoth cinema, air-cooled, air-conditioned, with seven hundred seats and a Wurlitzer organ to rise from the bowels of the orchestra pit, playing sugar music in lights of rainbow colours until it sank artistically down again with the last note.

'It will change colour in the lights,' Mr deSouza told them. 'Purple, red, orange and Prussian blue.'

'But the organist, he will change colour as well,' cried Blanche. 'Purple, red, orange and Prussian blue . . .'

'That can hardly be avoided,' said Mr deSouza stiffly. 'You must shift before the end of the month, Mr Lemarchant. We must start work at once; the house has to be entirely pulled down.'

'You can't pull down our house, it's where we live,' said Blanche.

'Every stick, every stone will be broken up.'

An agonizing thought had come to Blanche, she seemed to

shrink with fear. 'You can't break up Echo,' she whispered. 'Oh, Mr deSouza, you can't do that.'

'Not a crumb will be left for a bad little girl,' said Mr deSouza, chucking her under the chin. 'And the joke is, but I tell you this confidentially, Mr Lemarchant, they paid me so much compensation for the loss of the house that they wish to pull down, and it has been condemned already.'

'Condemned?'

'Yes, it was in a filthy state. No wonder you all had dysentery, so it's very lucky all round. Don't mention this to your friend Mr Bright. I don't wish him to know that the house will be broken up.'

'You are afraid because of the tablet,' said father. 'And what if I tell on you, what then, Mr deSouza? Oh, you have been a little too clever, I think.'

'There is,' said deSouza thoughtfully, 'that little matter of the rent you have not paid. That might be adjusted, and now my son Robert has told me that he and your girl Rosa – I smacked his head for it, but it is true, Mr Lemarchant – that they might be married. Robert can have something to do at the Paramount.'

'The Paramount?' asked father.

'That is to be the name of the cinema. Come with me, Mr Lemarchant, and I will tell you what I shall do.'

Blanche watched them walk away with despair in her heart.

'Father,' said Robert to Mr deSouza that evening, 'when they pull down the east wing ask them to be careful of the carving of the dog. They will be careful if you ask them.'

'No, no, it isn't safe. The tablet must be broken up or somebody might find it.'

'Just the dog, father. It's for the little girl. Give it to her.'

'Nothing of mine shall be given to that family that I can help.

Isn't it bad enough that you must bring that Rosa here, that I must give back to Joseph Lemarchant the rent I have earned? Tcha! Don't talk to me, Bob.'

Everyone was packing up, grumbling at Mr deSouza, but they were glad to go, to leave the rotten old place. The heat of September was gone, the October days were drawing to the cold weather; there were asters and early chrysanthemums in the flower market, already it was cool at night; they looked forward to starting the winter in a new place.

Robert and Rosa were to be married from the new flat, but all the excitement of it had gone. Father had no money for a wedding and Mr deSouza made a great to-do.

'You see how it is,' he said to his wife. 'My eldest son to get himself in such a fix. They would give a cheap, common show. I would be ashamed, so I must put hand to pocket as usual, and it is her Mr Bright I have to thank for this, but for him and his tablets I could snap my thumbs at them.'

Rosa seemed not to know or care, she was wrapped in a dream and now, when she looked at the tablet, she felt scornful of Rosabelle, the young girl in whose lap the unicorn might still be lulled to sleep. Robert had a thin, painful look, like the Jesus on auntie's crucifix, thought Blanche. She was sure he did not want to marry Rosa.

Auntie had no joy in it, only a great relief; she packed their things away in tin boxes and the wicker country stools called 'morahs'. She was glad to do it, for it was right that they should go, but it was wrong for a chapel to be pulled down to make a cinema. She put on one side the things that could be given to Rosa so that she should not be entirely shamed before the deSouzas. There was the silver ring on which Blanche had cut her teeth and a christening robe that she herself had made long ago when her hands were their proper size. She thought for a moment and put them for Rosa's baby with the other things.

She was the only one in the house with a sense of religion at all, Father Ghezzi had told her so. None of them, father, Belle, Rosa, had religion at all. Even Blanche from the very beginning: she remembered how, when Blanche was a child of three, she had taken her to the old Cathedral when the priest was saying Mass.

'Well, what did you see?' asked father when they came back.

'We saw God's house,' answered Blanche.

'Did you like it?'

'No,' said Blanche. 'The bells were ringing and God was shouting, I didn't like it at all.'

'Tst. Tst,' said auntie, wrapping the shoe polish in a pillow-case and putting it in a saucepan. 'They get bad blood from their father, no matter what they have discovered.'

Blanche came and sat on the lid of the trunk to help auntie close it; she seemed to have pink-eye, and her face was sodden with tears.

# 25

Now the house, that had been there since anyone could remember, stood open and empty in a fringe of rubbish and waste paper. Even the litter that the tenants had left when they went away had been picked over by the people from the street, people who spat on the floor and broke off the slats of the shutters for firewood. The crows and stray cats came timidly in to see what this sudden quiet might mean, and a sacred bull blundered its way through the door in the gate and for three days it could not get out; it ate the last of auntie's flowers and tore down the sorrowful jasmine. It's lowing could be heard all down the street and the people said it was a ghost and were afraid to go in.

Then half the front wall was knocked down to make a way for the bullock carts, and boards were hung across the gate; the coolies came with their baskets for carrying earth, the watchmen put up a house of matting against the wall and lit their fire on the drive.

As the house came down, the garden was buried in brick and rubbish, but first the palms were cut and carried away, and they fell one by one, with a sound like blows dealt on the back of the tottering house, and their heads, which for so long had whispered in the wind, were laid in the dust.

There were mounds of lime and brickdust and cement, and the bullocks with a string tied to their noses grazed on the grass that was left. On the back staircase that stood to the last fluttered a dish cloth; it caught the wind and waved there like a flag, and of all the people who had lived in the house there was no other sign; the deSouzas, the Bartons, Mr Kawashima, the Mascarenes and the Lemarchants were all gone.

The watchmen would not stay. The old story still ran in the bazaar and, watching tensely in the night, they said they saw the coach drive out through the gates, and a man, white-haired, white-faced, looked out at them, and all night in the house, given over now to the ghosts, they heard music and voices and someone who sobbed and cried.

Blanche came every evening, picking her way over the bricks. Her eyes felt dry and strained, and in her throat was such a lump that she could hardly breathe. She came when it was dark and the workmen had gone.

All these days she had tried to save Echo and she had failed. They were all against her, Robert and Rosa bound up in their own affairs, auntie who said, 'What nonsense, child,' father and Mr deSouza and the men, worse than devils to Blanche, who were destroying the house. They were all against her and she, pitifully, was a child.

On her way from school she always went to see, and there was Echo still unharmed on the wall. She had offered the foreman her silver bangles if he would save Echo for her.

'You can't get them off,' said the foreman.

'I can cut them off.'

'What use are they then to me?'

They would not come off. In the pantry with Boy she soaped her hands and set her lip and told him to pull them off.

The pain of crushing her hand through the small hoop of silver made her scream, but she told Boy not to take any notice, but to go on pulling.

'No, I daren't,' he said, 'the bones will break.' Her hands had swelled from the bruising and it was worse than before.

'Won't you take them for the silver?' she begged the foreman. 'Even if I cut them the silver will still be there.'

'They are not worth anything,' said the foreman rudely. 'You go home to your mother and leave us alone.'

'Then give me the dog. Give him to me and I shall go.'

'How shall I give what isn't mine?'

'You would if I had some baksheesh,' said Blanche bitterly.

'Give me five rupees.'

As well ask Blanche to find a hundred as five rupees. Even Boy would not give her money. They chased her away and would not let her come into the garden at all, but now it was evening with nobody there.

At this time the garden would have been quiet with shadows, the palms moving in the wind, rustling their leaves; if Blanche shut her eyes, almost she could hear them and smell the scent that came in through the windows when the jasmine was in flower and the moon was strong.

She could see again the windows with the curtains that did not match and the beds, hers and auntie's and Rosa's, even Belle's that had been taken away. There was the striped rug and the chest-of-drawers and auntie's table that she had made into an altar. It was a table again now in the new flat that Blanche hated; the things had gone there with them, the striped rug, the beds and the chest-of-drawers, but she had to leave Echo behind on the wall. Echo! She broke into a sob.

This was her home that they were breaking, where she had lived since she could remember. To other people now it was a jumble of brick and stone, but she knew every corner; here in this pile was the back of Mr Kawashima's pantry, here where the hat-stand had stood was still a part of the vestibule floor, this was the place where the sideboard had been, and this was the pillar where the cracks had made a face.

A desolation and despair filled her. Now she could trace where they had been, but soon, with the Paramount rising on their ruins, there would be nothing left.

'Where do you think Echo and the Lady will go then?' she had asked Robert.

'Well, I don't think they will like the Paramount, do you? Perhaps they will go to heaven,' he teased her.

'Auntie says dogs can't go to heaven.'

'I say they can.

'So do I,' said Blanche promptly. 'I wonder why he didn't go there before.'

'Those little dogs are very faithful,' suggested Robert, 'and I suppose he didn't like to desert his mistress, no matter what she chose to do, so he thought he would be a ghost, too.'

'Are they ghosts?'

'We have no other name for them. I wonder,' said Robert, 'what will happen now. Shall we see the Lady in the Paramount? Will she still be there? We might go and see.'

'We shall never go there,' said Rosa, 'never, and yet,' she added, 'perhaps in a way we shall. If Belle is shown there on the films, Bob, that would be a strange ending, wouldn't it?'

Blanche waited in the ruined garden until the light had

nearly gone and the dusk made queer shapes and shadows among the stones. She had found nothing of Echo, her hands were sore from turning over bricks and rubble; she was still weak from the dysentery and her back ached; there seemed to be faces peering at her and odd animal rustlings. Furtively she got up to go, feeling her way round the garden away from the ruined house.

She stumbled and nearly cried out; she had fallen over a stone shape that lay on the ground. The light from the street lamp came dimly over the wall and she saw that it was the sun-dial, lying broken, the jasmine withered to dried stalks and leaves like paper. It was broken at its plinth and its dial had rolled out of its setting on to the ground and was split into halves.

'How funny,' said Blanche, speaking to herself under her breath as auntie did. 'I never knew it could break; I thought it was *iron*.' And she remembered that Stephen had told her that before, that it was not iron but another metal, not copper, but something like that, she could not remember the name. She bent down to see, and to her surprise it was not broken at all, it must have been meant to come apart, for there on the two edges were little metal teeth that fitted into one another and locked just as she could lock her fingers together. She saw how they had been jerked apart when the sundial fell. 'I wonder if they always had to do that when they wanted to open it,' she said, for even to open her fingers if she held them together needed a jerk. She could not fit the dial together, for the halves were too heavy for her; but she could see that they had met in one of the grooves that marked the hours, so that the junction would be invisible both there and along the arm, where it would be hidden by the flowers and leaves that were chased along its edge.

Listlessly she sat on the ground and took one half on her lap; it was as cold and heavy as the feeling she had had inside her for weeks, and she sat there with it, resting her cheek on the point of the arm. It was uncomfortable, but it seemed to help the unhappiness, sharper now than the prick on her cheek, and she held it closer, running her finger along the toothed edge.

Suddenly she twisted herself round to the circle of light, for she had felt between the teeth a row of hard knobs like beads or peas in the edge; they moved a little under her finger and, scraped with her nail, one came out of its hollow like a pea out of its pod. It was coated with dirt but she scratched it, dreamily she wet her finger with her tongue and rubbed; the bead looked like glass or crystal cut into tiny edges, even through the dirt it sparkled in the light from the street lamp as she turned it this way and that.

She sat there dreamily with the bead in her hand, for she was tired, she let it drop from one hand to the other, not thinking, but with the shadow of Echo always in her mind.

There was a clang. Someone had opened the gate and was climbing across the brick towards her. Blanche sprang up, the dial rolled away; dodging behind the lime heaps, scrambling over the stones, barking her knees and tearing her dress in her haste, she gained the road. She was sobbing for breath, her knees were bleeding, and she had dropped the bead. 'Oh well,' she said, for she could not have shown it at home, if they found out where she had been there would be trouble, for auntie had said she was not to go after Echo and annoy Mr deSouza. She would have to go home quickly and get Boy to mend her frock. She set off down the dark street at a trot.

'Well, did you find anything?' asked Boy.

'Nothing,' said Blanche hopelessly.

# 26

Stephen had not thought that the Indian winter could be beautiful. He had had a revulsion from the country, all its romance had turned for him to sordidness, but now the land, flat and green under limpid skies, filled him again with delight.

He had been away, to Darjeeling, and beyond Darjeeling to Phalut, and it seemed that in the cold weather he had come back to a new place and a new feeling. The strangeness had gone, it was almost like home. The gardeners were bedding out sweet peas and lupins, snap-dragons, pansies, candytuft and mignonette, the grass-cutter whirred on the lawn and through the windows came the filtered sunlight of an English summer. The sky of baby blue had balloons and ribbons of cloud, on the maidan the grass was trimmed and rolled for polo.

There were tennis parties, golf with late teas by a fire, riding on Sunday mornings with brunch at Tolly or Jodhpur sitting out in the sun to keep warm; there was paper-chasing in the frosty dawn of Friday mornings, and there were proper dances at which one wore tails, and once again women were seen in gloves and stockings. The very thought of the hot weather was gone, he would not think about it, the strain and the uneasiness, the weariness; he thought they had all been a little mad. He did not want to think about it; he avoided any place where he might meet Rosa; it seemed to bring back that smell of graveyard earth that had clung to him in the cemetery in those days of rain.

He had been ill. The rages and worries of those weeks had turned inwards and burnt themselves out in fever and sweats and thirstiness and aching bones, and then the thought of Rosa had tormented him; she was the fever and the thirst, and as they sweated themselves away she was still there, a perpetual ache that he thought he would never lose. At night when the fever was bad he shouted for her, asked William to fetch her and thought that she was there, wanting him, begging him to love her, and he screamed to William to take her away.

William went out to Gray and fell into a chair; he was tired and uneasy.

'Perhaps he was right and all of us were wrong,' he said. 'We shouldn't have interfered. There are things we tamper with and afterwards wonder how the hell we dared.'

'Tcha!' said Gray. 'You want a drink. He's not dying, he's only rather ill. You were perfectly right, and he was a silly young ass.'

'I'm not sure,' said William.

That was what Catherine said: 'I'm not sure, Stephen,' and could have bitten out her tongue for saying it.

As soon as Stephen saw Catherine stepping down from the train at Howrah Station in the early hours of a Saturday morning he knew that it was Catherine and only Catherine whom he had ever loved. The newly discovered memory hit him like a blow. In the darkness of that December morning, in the murk and cold, in the smell of soot and train oil and coolie sweat, her sweetness came back to him, that quality of sweetness spiced with wit that was peculiarly her own. D. had said: 'Catherine is *really* one of the little girls, "sugar and spice and all things nice, that's what little girls are made of".' Funny that he should remember that now in his confusion. He had forgotten her, all these months he had forgotten her, and the thought of his treachery rushed over him so that he blushed and stammered.

She came up to him and took his hands and said: 'Stephen! It's really Stephen at last!' He saw a hint of laughter in her eyes and knew she had been told; at once he was filled with a hot childish resentment and the thought of Rosa came back to him. Then he saw her eyes searching his face. The laughter changed to a puzzlement, almost a fear, and she said, 'Stephen?' gently as if she were saying, 'What have they done to you, my poor love?' She pressed his hands, clinging to them before he turned to kiss D.

When he was with Catherine there was always that unspoken question, there was always Rosa. He was as much with the remembered Rosa as with the real Catherine.

'Aren't you going to tell me about it, Stephen?'

'Yes. Yes, of course I am, but it seems so long ago. I had lost it quite till—'

'Till?'

'Till you came.'

'I don't understand.'

'Nor do I, but being with you has made it worse. I have this feeling as powerful as if Rosa were a ghost, only I know she isn't dead. I mean I should know if she were. I can't explain how, but I know I should. I dream about her when I want to dream about you; she gets in the way all the time. It's as if I were being punished, but I don't think I did anything so terribly wrong. No worse than other people, and yet—'

'And yet,' prompted Catherine insistently.

'This feeling of guilt. I can't get rid of it. Like those stains of blood that won't wash off. William has it, too.'

'I'm sure he hasn't. Why, it was William who—' Catherine broke off.

'Yes, he used to, but he doesn't now. He's uneasy. You ask him. As if he weren't sure. There's something, something I'm trying to catch. Something I should know. There were so many things, Catherine. I'm worried.'

'You haven't seen her, Stephen?' Catherine's eyes were anxious.

'No. No. I wouldn't. I'd hate to. I tell you I'd lost it quite. In the hills I didn't think about her at all.'

In the hills, in the shining air of another world; air, cold and rare, that had pricked him into a precious awareness of life, when each breath was vivid and he hardly needed sleep. There on the borders of Sikkim the wind blew from the snows and the plains were an insignificant patch below the rampart hills.

The water came from the ice rivers, there were streaks of snow on the ground; he had long days alone with the porters and the headman Passang, alone on the slopes under a Himalayan sky, and nights in a rest house solitary in the wind.

It was Catherine, his pale gold girl, clear as the ice springs and snow winds, who had brought Rosa into his mind. Rosa haunted him, and now he knew that to lay the ghost he must tell Catherine, but that childish obstinacy held him.

'You must tell me, Stephen. You *must*.' The panic in her voice made him look up sharply.

With Catherine he had always felt inadequate; with her he was not the gay, conceited Stephen, he was an awkward boy, too earnestly in love to be graceful. She made a child of him, and now, with that childish terror in her words, she was suddenly the child. He knew that she loved him, she had come down to him, and at once he soared in the opposite direction. He grew up. He took her hand closely into his and began to tell her.

Even now he did not tell it very well. Catherine could never see Rosa as anything else but a doll, a little doll of clay that in the end broke into powder dry as pith; but the strange unfinished story, the dark child and Echo the dog, the pretty young man called Robert, the sister flaunting her way to England, the motto on the sundial and the crest on the windows, the tablet among the old unrecorded graves and the tablets in the chapel, the unicorn and the appearances of the Lady, these lived and thrilled in Stephen's stumbling words.

'It's after the first of December, Stephen, and you haven't gone back?'

He shook his head. 'Yet I've had this feeling for weeks, a kind of pull, pulling me back. As if something had happened. As if – I'd left something of myself behind.'

'Stephen,' Catherine put her other hand over his. 'Stephen, if you go back, let's go together. Take me with you. Let me see it too.'

He hesitated, looked down at their hands joined together and up at her face. 'Have you thought about Rosa?'

She would not meet his eyes. 'I'm sorry,' she said after a pause. 'Of course, it's impossible.'

'I don't want to hurt her more than I need. If she saw you it would hurt her very much. You're so lovely, you see.'

'What was she like?'

'She was rather like someone cut out of paper,' Stephen said slowly. 'Not real. She seems more than ever like that to me now.'

'Still I'm not sure about it, Stephen,' said Catherine almost against her will.

'You mean you and me and – her?'

'No. I mean about that cheque. The one you gave her.'

'But why?'

'Aren't you being a little – smug about it.'

'Smug?' Stephen was hurt and surprised. 'Catherine, she refused it, made me feel a clumsy brute, and then kept it and cashed it.'

'But did she? Would she? She doesn't sound the girl who would. She never tried to have any hold on you. When I ask you what she was like you say she doesn't seem real, she's like a ghost, like paper. She wouldn't do a thing like that. Anyone who would do that would have made a scene when you left her; would have run you for breach of promise and all kinds of things.'

'My good Lord! I never thought of that,' said Stephen.

'And you never thought of this: who did you make that cheque out to?'

'I don't remember. Yes I do. I thought she wouldn't have a banking account and made it out to "cash".'

'Then anyone could have cashed it?'

'Yes! Anyone! I bet it was her father, though. Catherine, what shall I do? What *can* I do? I must do something.'

'You could write and tell her,' said Catherine swiftly, 'but would it do any good? It would only begin it again. Hurt her more. It's over now, isn't it? Isn't it, Stephen?'

'Of course it is, but this makes me—'

'Makes you what?'

'Makes me,' Stephen turned to her, that urgency was in her voice again, 'makes me more in love with you than ever, if I possibly could be, which I couldn't. Funny that you're the only one of us all, including me, who has ever been fair to Rosa.'

'Then promise me,' she whispered, 'promise me you won't go back without me.'

But when he had left her in the Fort and drove back across the maidan he had an overwhelming desire to drive down that street off Chowringhee and step through the door in the gate into the garden, and look up at the house and hear the palm trees in the wind. Just to look, to be there again, not to speak to anyone. His resolution was slipping away, he turned the car at Plassey Gate towards Chowringhee.

He left the Fort sleeping in its walls in the winter moonlight, with the lights of the ships like frosty stars in the river; there were mists on the maidan, wreathes of it hovered across the road, and Stephen shivered. In Chowringhee, the boys were still running after the cars with balloons and roses and pornographic magazines, though it was nearly morning and the dawn was late.

At first Stephen thought he was in the wrong street; it was changed, something was changed; and with a throb of his heart he saw that the house was gone. A horrible moment of fear took him, fear of the supernatural; he was sick with fright and trembling and then, under his car lights, he saw the boards hung on the broken wall; and where once the house rose, tall and steep above its columns and palms, was a gaunt wall and a rubble of brick.

Stephen stood in the gap where the gate had been; inside it was silent, bare, utterly desolate, he could not trace where the drive had been, the porch, or the garden. One cassia tree still stood, close to him, and the wind moved its branches mournfully as though someone sighed.

The sound of wheels swept by him. There must be an echo, he thought, but his car was blocking the street and the wind of the hooves and the passing wheels went through his hair, and it was as if that phantom passage had left him melancholy and with a great foreboding.

In the stillness he heard sobbing, and scarcely breathing, his blood tingling, he stepped near to where the porch had been and the last pillar stood. There was a shadow of blue, and the wind in the solitary tree still sobbed, and as he looked the shadow moved, with a violet bloom like blue silk stained by moonlight, and a little dog gambolled out from the pile of brick, the plumes of its tail blown backward by the wind.

# 27

In the wreckage Blanche found a piece of Echo's tail, a feather on a fragment of stone.

They had broken him up with the banner and the brave little unicorn; the wreaths and the writing were gone, there was nothing of Rosabelle left, only this fragment of Echo.

Blanche knelt on the stones and searched in the rubble; not a line of his head, nor one small paw. Quivering, she laid down the fragment she had found.

'It's no use keeping that,' she said through her tears, and dusting her hands she went away.